The Stolen Girl

THE SEQUEL TO FORTUNE SMILES AS LOVE DIVIDES

MARGARET NYHON

WILLOW PRESS

Published by Willow Press

Author contact: margaretf@hotmail.co.nz

This is a work of fiction. Names, characters, places and incidents either are the product of the author's imagination or are used fictitiously and any resemblance to actual persons, living or dead, events or locales is entirely coincidental.

A catalogue record for this book is available from the National Library of New Zealand.

ISBN 978-0-473-70208-3 (paperback)

ISBN 978-0-473-70209-0 (EPUB)

Contents

Live for what today has to offer,
not for what yesterday has taken away.
Sadness gives you depth.
Happiness gives you height.

Life After Leila

Ten years had passed since the disappearance of Leila from Auckland Airport and it was now classed as a cold case. All avenues had been explored with no leads left to trace. The surveillance camera had caught all images of people entering the ladies' restroom and everyone but for one grey-haired lady and a child had been interviewed. This person had not been caught on any other footage in the terminal, which was a mystery. There were no leads as to who she might be and although images of her were posted around the country, no one had come forward.

All that was left was the blame game between family members. Leila was sorely missed by all those close to her and all these years later, the pain was still raw.

Reece, Leila's father, was the biggest loser in all this, as he had sent his partner to pick her up from the airport. She was caught up in a traffic jam, due to a motor accident blocking the main arterial route to the airport, so arrived an hour late. When she got there, she learned of Leila's disappearance. The airport staff were frantically searching for the little girl, but all was in vain. Leila's chaperone had been waiting with her suitcase just outside the ladies' while she went to the toilet, but as the minutes ticked by, she became worried, so walked in to see if she was okay. To her horror the little girl was nowhere to be seen. She had not seen her come out, so was bewildered as to what had happened. Now she had to justify to the authorities her actions in the past ten minutes. Did she take her eyes off the restroom entrance? The answer was yes, as several people had come up to her to ask advice as she was wearing her air hostess uniform, so she had pointed them in the right direction. This of course left her a candidate in the blame game.

The understanding between Reece and Lily was that he was to call her as soon as Leila arrived, to let her know she was safe. So, it was just assumed he was the one meeting her off the plane. But when Lily found out that it was Natalia who was sent to pick her up, she was furious. Once again Reece had reneged on his parental duties; there was always something else that came first.

This all meant the end of Reece and Natalia's relationship. He ended up having to sell his hotel to pay out his partner, so his fortune was halved. He was back in Dunedin a heart-broken man, as he had lost his only child. Her disappearance left him wondering why he hadn't taken more interest in her, but now it was too late. He even had moments when he wished his life was back to the days when he and Lily and the three children were all together. But as he thought about things he realised where it had all gone wrong. It was his determination to prove he could succeed in life after the shock of discovering he was not who he thought he was. As his adoptive parents were both in the medical profession, he could not understand why he was only of average intelligence. But when the truth came out about his birth parents being of lesser status, he was not going to let this stand in the way of proving himself to his friends and showing that he could make it with the best.

Now here he was, right back almost where he'd started, working as a hotel manager for his former boss. With the help of his colleagues, providing they would stand by him, he hoped his future would look a bit rosier. They were a formidable team once, so perhaps they be that team again.

Leila's disappearance played heavily on Lily's mind, and there wasn't a day went by that she didn't pray that her little girl would return. The twins, now aged thirteen years, missed her at the start, but as the months and years went by, she just became a memory. On her birthday they would celebrate with a cake and a photo of her on the table. Lily's life changed after that terrible day, and she had to reassess her values in life. Right at the top was Kennedy. She moved in with him as she needed his support and his love, to help get her through that heartbreaking period. The blame game raged for several months between her and Reece but, in the end, no one was a winner and they were both losers, so a truce was called between them. Their past was now behind them, and Reece was back living in their family home. It still hurt him to think his half-brother, Kennedy, had now become his ex-wife's partner and that he was the father of the twins.

Lily and Kennedy's love blossomed now that they were in a live-in relationship, and he loved the twins dearly. His hands-on approach in the home and with the care of the children allowed her to continue with her chosen career. Her partnership in the law firm was a financial success and now that she was a District Court judge, she had her own chambers in the building. Her dream had come to fruition due to Kennedy's support, as he remembered that way back at their quiz nights, when they first met, she was studying law and aspired to become a judge.

In the latter five years Kennedy had taken Mackenzie and Harrison with him on many occasions to Lincoln's place, as they were both interested in technology. This was brought about by the schools being in lockdown. While the Covid pandemic raged across the world and savaged the economy, it was the internet and the resulting work from home technology aids that helped various sectors, including education. Would learning radically change and become more technology intensive for the students? Perhaps this was the beginning for students to be able to study various modules in their own time and extend their horizons beyond the current school curriculums. Mackenzie was already working on the designing of clothes for her avatar. Although still very young, she could see through Lincoln's high-tech set-up that the virtual world was not too far off. She had inherited her father's savviness to focus on the changing world that had emerged from continual lockdowns. The virtual world was a place she could participate in, at any time in any physical reality. Kennedy was very proud of her, as was Lily.

Harrison, on the other hand, was into the gaming side of technology, so spent many hours masked up, in the gaming parlours and arcades, waiting to challenge other youngsters with the same energy as himself. He knew what games were popular and had a head start on most, as Lincoln's home tech set-up was right up there with the most modern devices.

Both Mackenzie and Harrison were five when Lily moved in with Kennedy, so he became a 'father' to them. With Reece off the scene they gravitated to Kennedy, so it became natural for them to think of him this way. It had not been explained to them that he was their biological dad, but that would happen one day in the future. Since Leila's disappearance Lily and Kennedy didn't see any urgency to change the situation, as it would just be another disruption in their young lives.

Lincoln knew of people having lost their jobs through Covid, especially the younger generation. It taught them to go online, especially gamers, as well as those looking to make money, so the virtual world became a popular destination. People were able to rely on it because it was consistent, as they could visit and use this world at any time they desired; it did not have a time limit!

The real world was not stable, what with lockdowns

and new viruses circulating the globe, and doom and gloom became part of everyday life, so people needed an escape. Lincoln stayed away from the outside world as he hated seeing people in masks. It reminded him of a faceless society; in fact he called them walking zombies. There had to be a better world, one where there were no viruses … and there was in his eyes: the virtual world. This is where he was choosing to live. His co-workers all worked from home as they didn't want to go back to driving in a polluted carbon-filled atmosphere, and they preferred the safety of their own homes.

Kennedy's attitude and outlook on life had changed when he realised Lily was the love of his life, but by the time he discovered this, she belong to Reece. It had taken him years to get over the fact that he had taken Lily against her will, while she was married to Reece. He loved her completely and just had to have her this way, as she was never going to belong to him. He was gentle with her apologising and declaring his love for her as he was stealing her dignity as well as her self-respect.

Then one day everything changed: first the affair then the twins, and now she was his. He filled her life with love like no other person could. He was gentle and understanding, allowing all the time in the world to caress her, making her feel special and wanted. From the first moment he came in contact with Lily, a warmth passed from her to him, sending arousing messages around his body, something that had never happened before. From then on, he stopped dating as he was an embarrassment to himself and his partners as his body completely shut down. Not a day passed that he didn't remember that extraordinary warmth and for years, he held on to that special something.

Then there was Amelia, who was Reece and Kennedy's half-sister. When Amelia came on the scene it helped mend a rift between these two former friends. She was thrilled to find she had two half-brothers, something that occurred only because of her father's estate passing through Lily's office; this was what led to the breakthrough. But, sadly, just after Leila's disappearance, Lily and Kennedy received a call from Amelia saying she was now living in Australia as she had met someone online. This was cause for alarm as she was a very wealthy young lady and would be a good catch for an unscrupulous fortune-seeker. Kennedy especially felt disappointed as he liked Amelia, another progeny from his mother's philandering days, adding to the already twisted family tree. But she was going to keep in touch and let them know how the romance was progressing. This was a relief to Kennedy.

Since becoming a District Court judge, Lily was handling a variety of cases. She loved her work, as no one day was the same and she was pleased that she could remain impartial towards the parties that stood before her. Her workload at home was made much easier since Kennedy had become her full-time partner, as he shared the home responsibilities – such a different scenario to when she was married to Reece. They still had the full-time nanny during the week, allowing them to work to five o'clock when need be. It meant someone was there for the twins when they came home from school. But most importantly, when the lockdowns occurred, she made sure they were doing their lessons via Zoom. Out of the lockdown, Mackenzie and Harrison had become ardent fans of the internet, so were pleased when Kennedy asked them to accompany him to Lincoln's home, as he had the ultimate set-up, the most modern technology that money could buy.

Now that Reece was back on the scene there were awkward moments between the twins and him, as now they called Kennedy 'Father'. They did not have the same rapport with Reece, even before he was told the truth about who their biological father was. He seemed to care only for Leila. Being the first born, he had more time to spend with her, and then his life became busy when the twins came along, so the constant noise and chatter irritated him when he returned home at night after a long day.

Lily had no misgivings about Reece and her parting, but it was now affecting him as he was on his own. He let her know every now and again that they once had a good relationship and he was regretting they weren't still together. She just let it blow over, as she knew he needed the backing of Lincoln and Kennedy, because he had suffered both financially and emotionally after Leila's disappearance, and his split with Natalia.

Today Reece and Kennedy were meeting at Lincoln's home. He was very strict as they entered his house. They had to give an account of their health and say whether they had been in anyone's company where Covid was possible. Lincoln had become paranoid about viruses and was tending towards the virtual world over the real one. It was like being back to the beginning, as the metaverse had to be clearly explained to Reece who had trouble figuring out NFTs when they became involved with them, so this was a whole new platform for him to traverse. Lincoln was very exact with his explanations, and to him it was everyday jargon but to Reece it was more complicated. He started, "Essentially the metaverse is a network of 3D virtual worlds that are focused on social interaction, meaning users can interact with each other, connect to friends, attend meetings and experience things they would in the real world. Are you following me, Reece?"

"Why are we going down this avenue?" Reece said.

"It is widely regarded as the next frontier of the Universe Internet, presenting substantial business and financial potential for technology industries and other businesses. We are looking at this for our next big investment. Kennedy and I have studied this and there seems to be an opening here for new punters who will take a gamble before it becomes 'out there'. We already have dealt in Bitcoin and Ethereum along with NFTs, so we have money in these wallets, thus giving us the nuts and bolts to begin. It is now just a matter of making the right decision as to what options are waiting for us." explained Lincoln.

Kennedy added, "We know there are companies who have metaverse accounts and deliver products to their customers in the virtual world. There is even land being sold in the virtual world, which is the area we are interested in. We know at the moment it is selling for $20 US per acre, so what do you think, Reece?"

He shrugged his shoulders; this was way above his thinking. "I'll go along with you guys; you seem to know what this is all about, so count me in." He desperately wanted to be part of their investment due to his fading fortune.

Today began with a phone call from Amelia in Australia. She told Lily and Kennedy everything was working out well with her new partner and she was happy. When Kennedy asked where she lived, there was some hesitation. "I have bought a campervan and we are cruising around Australia. Don't try calling me because I don't know where we will be, but I will keep in touch when I can." It was then Kennedy asked what her partner worked at, and he was concerned when he was told he wasn't working at the moment, which is why they decided to travel. This left him feeling suspicious: who had bought the van, was this guy on to a good thing, would this end in tears? Lily told him not to worry; it was Amelia's life and she had to live it as she chose! Kennedy didn't want to lose the family connection between them, and now that they had found each other, he wanted them to remain in touch. "Why did she suddenly up and leave?" he asked himself. "She never spoke about meeting someone on the internet. I am at a loss as to why she left so suddenly…"

Amelia

Amelia had bought herself a nice beachfront home on Seaworld Drive on the Gold Coast. She and Leila were within walking distance of Sea World, so they were close to all the excitement. Because Amelia was very wealthy, they led a life of outings and fun-filled adventures, along with long shopping sprees, as they both loved to dress up. Leila's previous life was soon forgotten amid all this new luxury. She was now a teenager, fourteen years old, she attended a private school and met other young girls who also led a privileged life. She was wise beyond her years thanks to Amelia's parenting, as she was a devoted mother. This was all Amelia dreamed of, to become a mother, to have a daughter she could love and who loved her in return. She had not experienced this as a child, as her mother had walked out on her and her twin brother when they were six years old.

Not long after her mother left, her brother Peter died, leaving a grieving father, who then focused all his love on Amelia. She used to climb into his bed to comfort him and they would cuddle each other. At aged six this was okay but as the years passed it was not. The hugs continued and as she grew into a teenager, other things began happening. She didn't think it was right, her body was changing, she was developing into a young woman so asked her father to stop touching her, as she felt he was invading her privacy. But it continued and she didn't know who to speak to, as she was frightened her father would be put in prison, then she would have no one.

Then one night while she was asleep, she was disturbed by someone taking down her pyjama pants, so she cried out, but was silenced by a hand covering her mouth. "It's okay, Amelia, it is me, your father." He continued doing what he set out to do, leaving a frightened little girl in tears and totally distraught. This continued for several years amid her pleas for him to stop. When she reached the age of sixteen, she left school and found a job as a receptionist with a live-in position, so she walked out of the family home. This was her escape from the sadistic life forced upon her by her father. It spelt freedom, but she had been abused and was left scarred, leading to a hatred of men. She knew she would never marry as she felt ashamed of herself, and she wanted no other man to ever do to her what she had endured from her father.

She loved her newfound freedom and met new people.

Her busy life took her mind away from the past, until one day her father turned up and tried to persuade her to return home. This was never going to happen. He even tried to buy her friendship, but now that the cycle was broken, that was where it finished, as did any respect she had for him.

Several years passed without any further contact with him, allowing Amelia to sort out her life, to try to put her past behind her, but it never left. Many times, she had been asked out by young men, but the requests always met with the same answer … sorry!

One day she received a call from a hospital to let her know her father was asking for her as he was gravely ill; in fact his time was near. Amelia had misgivings about going to see him, but as he was her only living kin, she plucked up the courage to visit him. A dreadful shock awaited her, as she didn't even recognise him. There in a bed lay a shrivelled little man sound asleep, so she sat in the chair by his bed and waited for him to stir. When he opened his eyes, tears fell from them when he saw his daughter before him. "Come and lie with me?" he asked her. She walked over to his bed and took his hand and told him, "No, Father, I will not lie with you, that was the past."

"But I loved you, Amelia. You are all I ever had. I have left you my estate, and all I ask is that you try and find your mother and share some of the money with her. I won many millions as well as my money, so you will be a very wealthy girl." His voice became inaudible, and his eyes closed. Amelia called the nurse who told her he was on his last breath, so she sat until his end came. A sudden relief overcome her, was she free at last, had her haunted past gone forever?

This is where she came in contact with Lily. She was the lawyer handling her father's estate. When Amelia learned of the value of her inheritance, it left her in shock. She knew he was in real estate, but the win he mentioned, she knew nothing about. Was it a big lotto win? During this first meeting with Lily, she told her about her father's last request, to find her mother. She didn't know where to start so Lily offered to help, as this was one of her specialities. This was when all was uncovered.

Now she was part of Lily and Kennedy's family, and in fact Kennedy was her half-brother as was Reece, so a friendship developed. It was while in the company of the children that the yearning to be a mother arose, but this would never happen as she could never have a relationship with a man. She wanted a daughter of her own, one she could love. This was where her love for Leila blossomed. She loved this little girl and the feelings were reciprocal. Here was the daughter she longed for but could never have ... or could she?

It was the night before Leila's departure to holiday with her father in Auckland and they were all gathered at Lily and Kennedy's home, for a little farewell party. Arrangements had been made weeks earlier so Amelia knew all the flight details and times of pick-up at the airport. She was prepared, she had the false passport for Leila and their flight tickets to Australia.

The next morning Amelia caught the first flight to Auckland so she would be there when Leila arrived. She had an hour before Leila touched down, so was totally organised. After her plane landed, she saw the hostess accompanying Leila to the ladies' where she waited outside with her charge's suitcase. Amelia followed and caught up with her in the toilets. She told Leila she had brought two new wigs, one for her and one for herself, so they put them on and walked hand in hand out of the restroom and made their way to the international airport.

"Where is Daddy?" asked Leila.

"Your daddy has Covid, so he asked me to take you for a little holiday until he is better. Mummy knows you are with me. We are going to Australia for a few days. Have you heard about Sea World? You will love it."

Leila was excited at the mention of Sea World as she knew about it.

The next week was fun filled for Leila, and she forgot what she had left behind as each day they did something new and exciting. Then came the day when she asked again when she was going to see her daddy. Amelia had it all worked out, "New Zealand has a Covid pandemic, so we are not allowed to fly back until it is over. We will buy a nice home and live together until it is safe for us to return. Tomorrow we will go house hunting and you can help me choose one."

Leila was excited as she had never been house hunting before. The next couple of days were spent looking at lovely homes and it was on Leila's say-so that they bought a home on a canal block, only a stone's throw from Sea

World. They shifted in and the days came and went, and the fun continued. Amelia enrolled Leila at a private girls' school, which she loved and she made many friends.

One day Amelia announced that soon the borders would be open but wondered whether Leila was ready to go back to New Zealand. For Leila, so many things had been forgotten about her other world; this was now her home and she didn't want to leave it. It would mean leaving her friends and Amelia, who she loved dearly. At the moment, they were puppy hunting, just another string to Amelia's bow, so excitement was building in that department. Amelia thought if she allowed Leila to have a puppy of her own, it would be another attachment she wouldn't be able to walk out on. All Amelia's dreams had come true, as she had her daughter (despite being stolen) and she bestowed so much love on her, hoping she would never want to leave. Every now and again little bits of Amelia's childhood came back to her, so no, it had not totally disappeared. She had no desire to take a partner as she still felt ashamed of herself for what had happened. The blame was not hers, but the shame was.

Several years had passed and Leila was now sixteen and considered herself an 'Aussie'. She spent many afternoons lying on sandy beaches with her friends, and now she was thinking of joining the surf lifesaving club. It wasn't long before she and her friends were learning lifesaving skills alongside other young tanned guys. Were they the drawcard? She had grown into a lovely outgoing teenager who was very popular and reliable when on beach patrol. She worked with a mentor who was an older man whom she trusted completely. Today it was Leila's turn to open the surf club rooms and get them set up for the first patrol, which came on duty at 8am. As she was setting up her mentor arrived and made her a cup of coffee, so they sat and talked.

The next thing she remembered was waking up in a strange place, lying on a mattress on the floor. She felt battered and bruised and her underwear had been removed. She was in shock; what was she doing here, what had happened? Then reality began to sink in. Was she a victim of rape? Who had it been and why? She struggled to get up; where was she? It wasn't until she looked out the tiny window that she realised she was in a boatshed, one of many built along the beachfront. She saw her knickers lying on the floor so picked them up and struggled into them. Leila was hurting inside and out; her head was reeling, and she felt as if she had been hit over the head with a baseball bat.

It was only when she realised her vision was impaired that she realised what had happened to her. She had been drugged. As she made her way to the door, she was surprised that it was unlocked, so she opened it to find the beach alive with bathers. Had anyone out there seen who brought her here? Where would she start? No, she just needed to get away from this place, as far away as possible. She had no idea of the time, but the sun was starting to disappear, telling her it was late afternoon, so she had lost the best part of a whole day. She knew the area as she recognised the boatsheds. She had seen them before, even admired them for their bright colours, but for now their charm had disappeared.

When Leila arrived home, she was there alone, so the first thing she did was run a shower to try to wash away what had happened. She then climbed into bed and sobbed her heart out, before falling asleep. This was where Amelia found her when she returned, and thinking she must have had a long day, left her to sleep on. When she didn't show up for breakfast, Amelia looked in on her, only to be told she wasn't well and that she would stay in bed. Today being Sunday, Amelia told her to rest as there was no college. At lunchtime Leila felt hungry so dragged herself out to the dining room and perched on a chair.

"How did your day go at the surf club?" asked Amelia.

Just the mention of the surf club brought tears to Leila's eyes, which didn't go unnoticed.

"Is something wrong, my pet?"

Leila told her that she was finishing with the lifesaving club.

"But you love it. What happened?"

Leila sat in silence, but the betrayal was too much and she burst into tears. Amelia went over and held her. "Please talk to me. It is hurting me to see you in this state."

Leila told her she had been drugged and then woke up in a boatshed hours later. This was Amelia's worst nightmare; had she been raped?

"Did anyone touch you?" she asked. When Leila told her that her underwear had been removed, Amelia knew then what had taken place.

"Who was at the clubhouse with you?"

Leila couldn't remember as the drugs had taken over.

"Oh, my darling, that is terrible. Thank God you don't remember anything … We will get through this together. We should report this to the police."

This brought a protest from Leila. "I don't want anyone to know this has happened. It must stay between us; this is our secret."

"But someone needs to be punished. It's a despicable crime and he needs to be locked up," answered an angry Amelia.

"I don't know who is responsible, so I am not going near the surf club again. Someone there will be looking at me and laughing behind my back and I won't know who it is, so I will stay away. I will go to university and bury myself in a career," said an adamant Leila.

"Leila, I have failed you. I'm so sorry," sobbed Amelia. With this her mind flashed back to her younger years and what she had endured. Now this had happened to her own little girl.

"It's not your fault, Mother. Don't blame yourself. We will just have to battle on and put the past behind us."

Amelia knew that was easier said than done, but at least Leila had someone to talk to and help her through it … unlike herself.

Several weeks passed and phone calls came in from the surf lifesaving club members, all wanting to know why she wasn't attending any practices. Leila wrote the club secretary a letter, saying she would not be coming back, as she was going to concentrate on a university career. She wanted to make a new circle of friends and move forward.

Suddenly she had grown up and realised her life had no purpose, but that was all about to change. Over the next few months Leila noticed she was putting on weight and was at a loss as to why. When she mentioned this to Amelia, she suggested they go to see a doctor.

Today was the day of the doctor's visit and they found out that Leila was pregnant. Neither had put this into the equation as it was the furthest thought from their minds. How had life changed so quickly? Leila was horrified but Amelia was secretly happy, as now she would become a mother all over again.

"This means I can't go to university," sighed a disappointed Leila. But this was soon ironed out when Amelia offered to look after the baby.

Leila finished attending college in the latter months of her pregnancy and took up Zoom lessons towards the end. Her life was in complete contrast to what it had been. As things churned over in her mind, she decided to become a lawyer so she could defend young girls against male predators. She wanted to see justice done to those men who ruined young girls' lives. Sometimes she wondered if she had done the right thing by letting her perpetrator off the hook, but she was one of the lucky ones, who had someone that cared and loved her. So many of the young girls had no backing, they were abandoned and forgotten by society and were even overlooked in the justice system.

The baby girl arrived before the beginning of the first semester, so Leila was happy about the timing. She had a quick labour and managed well, thanks to her mother

whom she loved dearly. They named their little girl
Willow. The father's name was left off the birth certificate
for obvious reasons. Leila managed her daughter and was
guided by Amelia, who was in her element. For someone
who didn't think motherhood was ever going to happen
now she had two girls to love.

Lincoln

The time had come for the lads to decide on their up-and-coming investment. Lincoln knew that gaming was the most dynamic and enjoyable entertainment available today, across all platforms. This had been aided by the expansion of metaverse platforms in recent years. He had heard through the technology world that Microsoft, the tech giant, had recently disclosed a plan to acquire 'Activision Blizzard', which is projected to be the largest gaming acquisition in history.

"Why is gaming so popular?" asked Reece.

Lincoln said, "The young people today have money and can purchase games, so they can match their intelligence by interacting with other gamers from around the world at any time, day or night. There are no time limitations, or shortage of eager beavers, who spend hours on gaming. It is what the new generation are growing up with; their lives are geared to the technology world. Look how many parents have all the tech gear in their homes, so to the children it is second nature. They themselves own iPhone, iPad, Nintendo and other gaming devices and can access the internet to play 'Minecraft' and many more games that just keep going for days. months, even years. There is never going to be an end as to where technology is going to take us in the future."

Lincoln himself was one of those tech-driven guys who was preferring to live in the virtual world rather than the real world.

While this was all new to Reece, he knew the future was harder to predict than ever, particularly in the case of social media which had the potential to expose all. He had experienced this in the hospitality industry where he had to contend with change. He didn't find it easy, but his perseverance managed to get him there in the end. This is why it was important for him to team up with Lincoln and Kennedy again. Although the closeness between them, particularly with Kennedy, had diminished somewhat, this had to be put aside, as he needed their expertise to get on the money wagon again. He envied Kennedy as he had the twins and now that his Leila was still missing, he was a broken man. He wondered each day if she was still alive, as now she would be twenty; in fact, a young woman who was oblivious as to her background. Much like he had experienced at that tender age.

As the meeting progressed, they decided to buy a large package of land in the metaverse that was up for sale in a new city that was being established. Lincoln had convinced Reece and Kennedy this was the right place to invest. "It may sit for the time being but down the track our wealth will build once again," Lincoln told them. He also mentioned he was busy on another project; he was creating a new online game in which avatars could battle out the unrest between countries and their opposition, in ownership and war. He hoped the younger tech nerds might find a solution to deal with this disruption that was plaguing the headline news. Would they find a solution? Only time would tell.

Lily's life was hectic since she became a District Court judge. She was inundated with new cases every day, so had backlogs of unheard cases, which she was receiving criticism about. Everyone wanted their hearing to happen immediately, but the courts were flooded with cases waiting to be heard. Not a day went by that she didn't think about Leila and wondered what sort of young lady she had grown into. She never thought for a minute that she wasn't alive; she couldn't live with that. Mackenzie and Harrison rarely talked about her any more, as it seemed a lifetime to them since she had disappeared. It was only the photo on the dining room dresser that kept their sister's memory alive.

Lily and Kennedy had still not discussed with the twins who their biological father was, but the time was nearing for them to hear the truth. She was still as much in love with Kennedy today as when their affair first started. She did, however, have moments when she thought back to her marriage to Reece, realising his feelings were not a match for Kennedy's, but at the time they seemed to fill her needs. So much water had passed under the bridge and she was thankful that Kennedy had come into her life, although it was an unorthodox start. As time passed, she realised that his love for her, over several years, had plagued him before the incident. He made her feel good about herself which helped restore her faith, as she copped a lot of flak from courtroom dramas. She loved Kennedy making love to her; his consideration for her feelings were foremost, along with the caressing and sweet talk. It was a confidence boost that enabled her to cope with outbursts during her court cases. He was a wonderful father to Mackenzie and Harrison. They loved him dearly as he was always there for them, right from when they were babies.

Today Lily was facing her most dreaded case, as it brought home feelings that were close to her heart. A father had absconded, taking with him his two daughters and leaving a distressed mother. The police had managed to contact him in Australia where he was settled in with a new partner and his daughters. The case had taken eighteen months to come before the District Court, so the girls had got used to a new life, one that they didn't want to leave. Meanwhile back in New Zealand a broken-hearted mother was prepared to fight to get her girls back. As the girls were younger than sixteen, they could not make the call to stay with their father. As it was now a case before the District Court, the judge would make the final ruling.

Lily had requested the girls attend her chambers so she could interview them without the guidance of either parent. They were aged seven and nine years, very pleasant and knew where they wanted to live. They liked their father's new partner, as she left all the decision making to the girls and to their father.

"Don't you miss your mother? She is devastated that you live away from her. Think how lonely she feels without you both," said Lily. The girls looked at each other, waiting for either one to speak. It was the nine-year-old who spoke, "Mum and Dad were always fighting. Simone and Dad never fight and they are happy. We don't have to choose any more. We want to stay with them."

This was like a dagger stabbing Lily's heart; how would she feel if this was Leila saying these things? She spoke again. "But your life would be different at home now that your mother and father don't live together any more. There would be no fighting so you wouldn't have to choose. Your mother loves you both and misses you, she wants you to come back and live with her. How would you feel about living with her and having your school holidays in Australia with your father? That way they would both have time with you. You must remember your mother has no one, and she needs you."

Lily had to remember her duty as a judge, to always remain impartial.

"Your father took you away without your mother's

consent and she worried about you as she didn't know where you were. Tell me what you think now?"

She saw tears in their eyes as they listened and hung their heads. Neither spoke. Lily didn't have to think to make her decision. "I want you both to come home and live with your mother, then you can visit your father in the school holidays. I will call in on you after two months and make sure you are happy. I will inform your father of my decision. Thank you, girls, I'm sorry it had to come to this, but in the end, it is my decision as a judge to ensure I have acted in the best interest of all parties. Take care, bye for now."

The girls left without protest, which made Lily think they were quite happy with the outcome. Now she had the task of informing the father. He was not happy, but this was her ruling, therefore it had to be abided by.

That night Lily sat with Mackenzie and Harrison and explained the day's happenings. They knew they could not repeat anything their mother told them if it involved her court work. She felt she just needed to share this with them as she felt moved deep within, simply because Leila was etched in her mind.

"Do you think Leila might be living in Australia?" asked Mackenzie.

"What made you ask that?" said Lily.

"It just came to my mind."

On this note they all said goodnight and went to their rooms. As she and Kennedy were getting ready for bed Lily broke down and started to sob, as today had been playing on her mind and her emotions needed to be let out.

"What is wrong, my darling?" he asked.

Lily explained her feelings of sadness when she thought about Leila and her case today had brought it all to the fore. "You know, Kennedy, I still miss her so much; she was my first born. It tears at my heart not knowing where she is, but I know in my own heart she is out there somewhere," she sobbed.

Kennedy understood how she felt, as he too missed her. They had a special bond although he was not her biological father. "Come to bed, my darling, and let me hold you. Together we will get through this."

As Lily climbed into bed, she felt Kennedy's arms enfolding her. He had something on his mind that he wanted to share with her. "Lily, do you realise we haven 't heard from Amelia for several months. I hope nothing has happened to her relationship. We don't even have her cell phone number so we can't make contact with her. I can't understand why she hasn't given it to us. We will just have to wait until she contacts us next. I never want us to become strangers again."

Lily turned to face him and tenderly kissed his cheek. "If we don't hear from her, I will do a search and see what I can find out. Let us make love and forget all else. Let there just be you and me in our own little world tonight."

Kennedy didn't take any prompting and his body was ready to respond, as this was the effect Lily had on him, right from when they first touched all those years ago. She radiated a warmth he had never experienced before and had never forgotten; he had to have her. Although it took its time to manifest, he had acted on his own bodily needs without her consent. The saving grace had been that he was gentle with her and amid his apologies, he had kept declaring his love for her.

But with all these memories behind her, he was the ultimate lover. It was the caressing and sweet talk that Lily loved, as there had never been any foreplay in her marriage to Reece, so these were treasured moments. He took his time to please her, and in the end, it was Lily who begged to be taken. Fortunately, he could hold off until she was ready, then the fireworks! To become as one was the ultimate and this sealed their love for each other.

In the post today came an official-looking letter with a government stamp. Lily was excited and tore it open to see what news it held. To her utter joy, it was news she had worked all her life for: she had been appointed as a High Court judge. The position was Lily's to accept or decline, there was no thinking needed.

Her ultimate dream had been realised. It had taken longer than she anticipated to reach this goal, but here it was! The reason for the long wait was for a reigning judge to stand down, as there are only forty High Court judges including the Chief Justice in New Zealand. Judges stay in their roles for long periods and these positions are highly sought after by lawyers, so this was no mean feat for Lily.

On further reflection, she had not taken in all the details in the letter so reread it. The position would become vacant in two months' time and fortunately it was in Dunedin, so no upheaval for the family. So many questions flooded her mind: could she manage all the cases waiting to be heard in that two-month period? No, that was not possible, and they would have to be heard by her successor. One thing for sure, her workload would not be as busy as being a High Court judge, as she didn't have to cover so many facets of the law. Her work hours wouldn't be from 8 o'clock to 5 o'clock as there would be nights involved, if there was a verdict to be reached. Also, there were four terms in a legal year, which are main sitting times for the High Court and Court of Appeal. This was a new challenge for Lily, but one she was prepared to face with open arms.

Harrison was now seventeen and right into gaming technology. He was Lincoln's right-hand man as he had first-hand knowledge of what the kids wanted and what they were buying. He spent all his spare time on computers, linking up with like-minded enthusiasts from all around the world. Lily and Kennedy had to take control of his screen time as through the virtual world he could play games 24/7. This was where the danger lay!

First and foremost the kids of today wanted action; guns and bombs were number one as they tended to like killing fields. Avatars had become the ones fighting the battles as they were controlled by the players. In this unrealistic world, subjects would be shot but were still able to battle on, something very entertaining for the players who were seeking excitement without any consequences.

In the real world if one was shot, they died, but this was not so with virtual reality. Was this why the nerds preferred to live in a world where one just picked themselves up and carried on trying to better themselves … with no consequences? But this didn't happen in the real world. Just as well Harrison's time was vetted, as he was well on the way to becoming another statistic, lost to virtual reality. He did not play any sport although he was encouraged to do so. It held no appeal for him, as it was time wasted in his mind. He had taken an IT course in computer programming so he could develop his technology skills hoping one day to be rich, as he had a combination of his parents' intelligence and determination.

All this was being watched by Reece who was envious of his half-brother, as Kennedy had it all, including his ex-wife and the twins. All he had was a broken heart and a half-emptied bank account. He had never picked himself up after the loss of his daughter. Unlike Lily, he had given up hope of her ever coming home. Oh, how he wished he could go back to his old life, when he and Lily were husband and wife. If only he had played a bigger part in her ambition to become a High Court judge; instead he tried to put obstacles in her way.

He shuddered to think he didn't even share some of his crypto wealth to help Lily buy a share in the law firm, as now she owned it outright. She was a very wealthy woman. It wasn't until they parted that he learnt that Kennedy had put up the money for Lily to buy a share in the firm. This left bitter feelings towards his half-brother, but he knew if he wanted to replenish his wealth, these feelings would have to be put aside.

Originally it was Reece's money that got them started, but now they were millionaires in their own rights, they could cast him aside. But this was never going to happen, as Lincoln and Kennedy would never forget how they got to where they were today.

His flash-in-the-pan affair with Natalia, he had since worked out, was more for companionship, as they both loved the hospitality industry. This is where it all went wrong with Lily, as he had just expected her to fall in line with his career, forgetting she had one of her own. If he hadn't been so pig-headed, they could have worked something out, but that was past tense. All he could do now was watch the blossoming relationship between Lily and Kennedy. This hurt Reece right to the core; he was jealous and longed to have her back in his arms. Lily was a success story: she owned her own law firm and her salary as a High Court judge was $525,000, a tenure that could not be decreased, to ensure judges remained impartial.

How he wished he had gone on this journey with her, but it was too late. All he was left with was memories of their quiz nights, how they first met, Lily with her hair tied back and wearing a beret, a law student who had set herself a goal.

Reece

The travel agent was finalising Reece's airfares from Dunedin to Melbourne, then on to Alice Springs. Reece had been thinking a lot about his parents lately. He felt now was the right time for him to go back and visit their last living memory. It seemed so long ago since that day when he learned of their deaths; they were his parents and he loved them dearly. Although they were not his biological parents, they were the ones that brought him up and loved him completely. They never wanted him to know he was adopted, and it was only by a slip of the tongue from his aunty that he learned the truth. It hurt for a while, but as the happy memories of his childhood came flooding back, the hurt was short lived.

Reece flew into Alice Springs and hailed a taxi to take him to the motels where his parents and uncle and aunty had stayed. He hoped the pain he felt then was not going to be felt again. He vividly remembered the motel entrance and asked the taxi driver to let him out. He carried his bags across the lawn to reception. Once settled in, he took off his shoes and lay on the bed, letting his mind take him wherever. He felt an overwhelming warmth flow through his body, something he hadn't felt for a long time; had he finally accepted that his parents were at peace? He knew his mother had wished to see Uluru and it was the last place she wanted to visit, but little did she know it would be where her life was going to end. Reece had made a promise to himself to stand on the very spot the accident happened.

First, he went to the flight office and introduced himself and stated why he was there. The company agreed to drive him to the crash site, as they had laid a stone in memory of their pilot and his passengers who perished that fateful day. It was a good two-hour drive, so he had plenty of time to think what feelings this journey would stir within his body. The driver, also a pilot, remembered the talk of that fateful day as it was their last fatality. The company had learnt its lesson, as the authorities had come down hard on them and there was the large compensation payment made to Reece.

As they neared the site, Uluru came into view and he could understand why his mother had this on her bucket list. It was truly magnificent. He hadn't visited here when he came to collect their bodies as everything was still raw. Now he was ready. They pulled up beside a grassed area where a plaque had been laid in memory of those who perished at this very spot. Reece climbed out and walked over to the plaque and knelt beside it. As his fingers traced the outline of his parents' names, tears rolled down his cheeks, and he was not prepared for the outburst of sorrow that followed. Was this the letting go? The driver walked back to his vehicle as he could see how stressed his passenger was; he knew he needed to be left alone to grieve.

On his way home from Alice Springs, Reece decided to stop off at the Gold Coast as he still had another week of holidays. He had never been to Sea World, so this was as good a reason as any to finally visit. He was booked into the Marina Mirage on Seaworld Drive as it was near the popular theme park. Today was Saturday so it would be a busy day at the park but that was part of the attraction, to mix and mingle with the crowd. Reece loved the buzz from being among lots of people. As he walked around, he saw a couple of rides that he thought he was brave enough to go on, but it was the roller-coaster that frightened him most. It reminded him of his parents' death, so he would stay away from it.

Hunger took over as he walked past a hot-dog stand, so he bought a hot-dog and a pottle of chips and walked to a park-like area where people were sitting on the ground enjoying their lunch. As he was eating, a little girl came toddling over, and took a chip from his pottle. Suddenly her mother came over and apologised. "I'm so sorry." Reece said it was okay and not to worry.

"Are you a tourist or a local?" he asked.

"Oh, I live here; in fact just nearby. My daughter and I come here every Saturday as I am at university all week."

"What are you studying?" Reece asked.

"I am a law student; I want to be a lawyer."

For a moment he was taken back in time, as that was what Lily told him when they first met. "Are either of your parents' lawyers?" he asked. With this question came a silence, so Reece apologised for asking too many questions.

"Don't apologise. I want to be able to help defend young girls who have been taken advantage of." Reece let her know he thought that was a noble gesture to protect vulnerable girls. As he thought about this, he did wonder if she had in fact been abused, as she seemed young to be a mother, but then this was Australia! As she started to walk away Reece asked if he could take a photo of the two of them, but this met with a flat refusal. He thanked them and said goodbye, then carried on. He was a bit surprised, but perhaps she thought he was intruding on her life. It was time to head over to see the dolphins performing. The show was about to start so the pool area was packed with people. The dolphins delighted the crowds and cameras were flashing from all angles, even he was snapping away.

That night back in his hotel suite Reece was browsing through the photos he had taken of the dolphins and was surprised to find he had captured the young lady he was talking to and her daughter. They were in the second row opposite him, not that he had noticed them at the time. He had mixed emotions as he didn't have her consent; would she be upset? He pondered over the photo. Why did he feel this way, was he thinking of Leila, was this what she would look like if she was still alive? Reece decided to get this image printed, so tomorrow that would be the first thing on his agenda. He couldn't get her out of his mind; was it because she was studying law, just like Lily when they first met? Was it nostalgia he was holding onto, as his love for Lily was still haunting him?

Two hours after handing in his photos to be printed he went back to collect them. The young assistant was very chatty and asked Reece where he was from. As he was checking the photos, he showed the one with the young lady to the assistant and asked if she knew of her, as she had said she lived nearby.

"Why yes, that's Lee Lee. We joined lifesaving classes together, then one day she never came back. We wondered what was wrong, but then we heard something terrible had happened to her. Apparently, she is at university studying law. She has a little girl who her mother looks after while she is studying."

The name Lee Lee took him by surprise. "Lee Lee, that's an unusual name, what is it short for?" Reece asked.

"We have only known her by that name, so I don't know."

He thanked the salesperson and went on his way. He couldn't get the name out of his head; it was so much like Leila.

Reece went back to Sea World hoping to catch up with the stranger once again. Although he knew she attended university during the week, he hoped perhaps she may have had an afternoon off, but this was not to be. Sadly he would be back in New Zealand by next Saturday, so he would not catch up with her before he left. He just could not let go of the thought of Leila. Were they about the same age? No that was impossible, as the stranger had a child. Leila would not be of age to have a daughter, but of course she could if she had been raped, as age didn't come into it.

At home, in Dunedin, Reece had started back at work at his hotel, much to the delight of his staff. They missed him, as the relief manager was not as personal as Reece, so they couldn't wait to see him move on. As he thought back over his holiday, he remembered his parents' plaque, Uluru and the stranger. But it was the stranger that held most of his interest, especially since hearing her name, which was so close to Leila. He had her photo in his wallet, which he took out and looked at often. Next time he met up with Lily, he would show her the photo and see what she thought.

He couldn't wait to catch up with the lads again and see what had been happening in the financial world while he was on holiday. He knew Lincoln would be right up with the play in the virtual world, and then there was Kennedy, his arch-rival, but this had to put on the backburner as he was the financial whizz. They were a good team together and he needed them.

A meeting was arranged for 7.30 that night after Reece finished work. Lincoln worked from home and Kennedy could take time off whenever, as he was now CEO of the finance company. Reece had read an interesting article in a Melbourne financial paper, so he had torn it out and put it in his wallet to read to the guys at their next meeting, so that was tonight.

The first topic of conversation that arose was Reece's holiday, as the lads were hoping he might have had a holiday romance or met someone special, but no, this did not happen. He took out the cutting and began to read it to them. "The pandemic has opened our eyes to certain solutions and broadened our perspective on some technical issues – not to be afraid of functioning in a remote world, as this is our future world. Virtual reality technology has not yet crossed into mainstream, but it is certainly knocking on the door."

Before anyone had a chance to respond, Lincoln stood up. "A truer word has never been spoken, that is why we must look to the future and choose the right path, as there is money to be made, and plenty of it, so let that be us lads. We already own virtual land, and Harrison and I know that gaming is where the money lies. He is young and mixes with the gaming crowds, so he can give us first-hand information. Are you with me on this?" The silence was broken by a firm yes by Reece and Kennedy.

"Will you agree for Harrison to come to our next meeting, as he is our key to the gaming world?"

That night Kennedy went home feeling proud that Harrison was considered a helping hand on future decisions to be made for the lads. He couldn't wait to tell Lily and Mackenzie. Mackenzie had been on the computer looking for clothes for her avatar, as new fashion houses were popping up vying for sales. All the top fashion houses were branching into the metaverse, which was where the future lay as punters wanted to dress their avatars to replicate themselves. This didn't come cheap!

Mackenzie was studying journalism as she wanted to interview people who were making a difference to others' lives. This was brought on by some of her mother's cases that she was privy to, as she had pleaded with Lily to take her to the courtroom several times, to listen to interesting cases.

As Kennedy was telling the family about Harrison's good fortune the telephone rang. Kennedy answered and was surprised to hear Amelia's voice. "Hi, why has it been so long since you called us? We were worried about you. Is everything okay?"

She assured them that all was great with her, the love affair was going strong and they were still travelling around Australia in their motorhome.

"We were thinking of coming to Aussie to visit you soon. Where will we find you?" Kennedy asked. There was some hesitation.

"I can't give you any timeframe as we don't know where we will be tomorrow; it depends on casual work. Don't worry about me. Everything is fine and I'm happy."

Kennedy asked where they were staying now.

"We are on the coast at Forster-Tuncurry. My man has a job as a stand-in maintenance man at a resort, so we will be here until the full-time guy returns."

"Well, give us your cell phone number so we can call you. We worry when we don't hear from you, and that will put us at ease," said Kennedy.

With this Lily came to the phone. "Hi Amelia, the boys

have been worried about you. Please contact us more; in fact if we had your phone number, we could call you."

This was met with a little resistance and the subject was changed. "How are the children? I miss them?"

Lily told her about Harrison and Mackenzie, but felt she had to mention Leila. "I really miss her, and not a day goes by that I don't think about her. I know in my own mind that she is out there somewhere. We will find her one day and bring her home." The phone went silent.

"I have to go now as someone is calling me. I will call you again soon." Then the phone went dead.

"That was short and sharp," remarked Kennedy. "We didn't get her phone number in the end. Why is she so elusive about giving it to us? Do you think she is trying to fob us off? Perhaps all is not well with the love affair?"

Lily was as baffled as Kennedy.

That night as they lay in bed the subject of Amelia came up again. "What if anything happened here and we had to get in touch with her, where would we start? It is not very good that we don't have her phone number," said Kennedy.

Lily told him not to worry, as there were more important things to do in bed. With this she turned to him and ran her hands down his back, caressing him until her hands slipped further down his body. He was still in fine form; he kept himself fit and toned. Not like Lily, as her body had not fully returned to normal since having the children. But she liked who she was, and this was due to Kennedy's love for her, as he always made her feel special, which gave her the self-confidence she deserved. Her hands stopped as she felt his proud body part, and she knew then he was ready to make love. But for Kennedy it was not all about him. He wanted to caress Lily's body to make her writhe in pleasure before they came together. This was what made him a great lover; he was prepared to wait until the time was right for both their bodies to ache for each other, then it was all on. Total exhaustion was the result.

At lunchtime Lily was surprised to find Reece waiting outside her law firm building. He had not stepped back inside since the day he verbally attacked her, after seeing her name as a partner in the business. "Hi Reece, what are you doing here?" she asked.

He asked if they could have lunch together. Lily thought this most unusual but agreed. They found an outside table at the little café across from where Lily worked, a place she frequented. After ordering something to eat, she couldn't wait to see what this meeting was all about. "Is something wrong?" she asked.

Reece was a little annoyed by this question as they were once lovers, married and now separated; couldn't they just meet without something being wrong? "You know I miss you Lily. I wish we could go back in our lives; things would be different second time around."

"But sadly, we don't get a second time, Reece. It is meant to work the first time ... and it didn't. I fell in love with Kennedy in the end, which is hard to believe, considering I thought he was an arrogant prick at the start. People change, you changed, he changed and so did I. Then when we lost our daughter that was the beginning of the end. No one knew this was going to happen, but the one thing I can never forget is our beautiful Leila. I miss her every day."

"That's why I am here, Lily, I want to talk about her." He went on to explain about meeting the young lady and her daughter at Sea World and what conversation followed. "There was something about her that made me feel close to her, even more so when I found out her name was Lee Lee. I have a photo I want you to see, then tell me what you think. It is the lady in the second row with the little girl. He watched her face to see her reaction. Then he noticed a tear fall on to her cheek.

"Oh Reece, that's just how I pictured Leila to look like today, but the little girl … are you sure it is her daughter? She is so young."

He then told her what the girl from the photo shop had said, that something bad had happened to her. "In my own mind I think she may have been raped. But the biggest surprise was when I learned she was studying law. I asked her why and she told me she wanted to protect young girls from male predators."

On hearing this Lily burst into tears. If this was their Leila how dreadful that something so horrendous had happened. Reece reached out and held her hand. "Lily, why do I feel a connection to this person? Please help me. I can't forget her image – it is with me all the time."

Lily still held the photo in her hand. "What if this was our little girl? We would be grandparents. She is beautiful, but this is coincidence, and I think we are presuming something that is not possible. What else do you know about this person?"

Reece told Lily she lived near Sea World and her mother looked after the little girl while she attended university. There didn't seem to be a father on the scene.

"How I wish this was real," said Lily. "Oh, Reece, one day we will find her, I know this in my own heart."

With these thoughts they stood up and hugged each other. To Lily this was a spur of the moment happening but to Reece it meant much more; could he win her back? If this was Leila, would things go back to what they once were? He had high hopes.

Lily was thankful she had a quiet afternoon at work, as she kept looking at the photo sitting on her desk. Reece had reluctantly let her have it, so tonight she would ask Kennedy to get someone to Photoshop the other faces out of the photo, leaving only the young lady and her daughter. Perhaps this would shed a new light on things. The rest of the afternoon was spent in dreamland, wondering what Leila would look like today. Perhaps she could employ a professional forensic artist to use their skills to create an image of Leila as an older person. Another choice was using the StyleGan tool that generates images of non-existent people. Because of Lily's work, she knew this had been used previously in different cases. She would talk with Kennedy about this.

In the evening, Lily sat the family down at the table and asked them to look at the photo she had in her hand. She said nothing about the image, but just wanted them to study it. She hadn't even told Kennedy about her meeting with Reece. First to look was Mackenzie, and at the start all she saw were the dolphins then she was drawn to a face in the audience. She stared at it; she thought she knew the face, but no, she didn't know anyone in Australia. On the billboard was the name 'Sea World' so she presumed it was taken in Aussie. She handed it on to Harrison to have a look, but all he saw was the dolphins, and people's faces didn't mean much to him. Next was Kennedy. He looked at the dolphins but like Mackenzie he noticed a face he thought he knew: the girl in the second row, where had he seen her before? He then asked Lily why they were looking at the photo; did they know anyone?

Lily told them why she had the photo and the story behind it. Mackenzie was the first to speak. "That is just what I expected Leila to look like, the girl in the second row, is that why I thought I knew her?" she asked.

Kennedy felt the same and was sure he had seen her before. Was it how he pictured Leila to look like also? But who was the little girl?

When Lily told them what the girl at the photo shop had told Reece, they were in disbelief. Mackenzie started to cry. "What if that is Leila, and that did happen to her, can we find out more about this person? Does she live in Surfers Paradise?" she asked.

The sun was shining, and it was a beautiful day on the Gold Coast, so Leila suggested they go for a walk and take Willow to the beach. She went to her bedroom and grabbed her camera to get some photos of her playing in the sand. She didn't often walk along the beach as it brought back memories of waking up in the boatshed. They saw the surf lifesaving club in the distance and were surprised to see so many cars parked there. Leila had never been near the clubrooms as she felt embarrassed.

They spent a lovely afternoon watching Willow who loved the sand. It was all through her hair as she threw it up in the air, so the camera worked overtime. On the way home they stopped off at the photo shop and Leila took the card from her camera and gave it to the assistant, who she knew from her lifesaving days. "Hi Lee Lee, I haven't seen you for ages. I hear you are at university. Did you know our lifesaving mentor has passed away? They are holding his service at the clubrooms today. I'm going along later."

"We saw the cars there as we passed and wondered what was happening. Yes, I am at university and loving it. You know my mother, and this is Willow," replied Leila.

The assistant suddenly remembered about the man who had asked if she knew who the girl in the photo was, so elected to tell her. "One day a man came in to get some photos developed that he had taken at Sea World. The particular one he asked about was one he took at the dolphins' performance, as you and the little girl were in the background. He asked if I knew you."

"I wonder if that was the man who spoke with me at Sea World. He asked several questions, but I had no idea where he was from," replied Leila. The shop assistant told them he was from New Zealand. Just the mention of New Zealand sent Amelia into a panic. "You didn't tell me about talking to a stranger; how did you meet him?" she asked.

Leila mentioned that Willow had stolen a chip from his pottle, so she apologised for her daughter's behaviour, and that was how the conversation began.

This explanation calmed Amelia down, but not enough to drop the subject. "Was he with someone and what did he look like?"

Leila explained that he was on his own, but he did ask to take a photo, which she declined. "I thought it was a strange thing to ask. Perhaps the photo he took was of the dolphins and we just happened to be seated in the background," she explained. Again, Amelia felt panic coming on; she just had to know if he asked where she lived.

"No, I told him I was studying law and he asked if either of my parents were lawyers." This brought on a new bout of fear as Leila's mother was a lawyer. Who was this nosey parker? Was she being paranoid when she didn't need to be? The shop assistant put Amelia at ease when she told them he was leaving the day after he picked up his photos and that was two weeks ago.

Several months had passed since the photo incident and life was back to normal. Amelia felt relaxed, although she couldn't bear the thought of losing Leila and Willow, as they were her life. In the post today came an official-looking envelope addressed to Leila and on the back was a stamp with a solicitor's address. She wondered why they would be writing to her. When she came home from varsity Amelia gave her the letter. She opened it then sat down to read. Amelia looked on as suddenly the colour drained from Leila's cheeks and she turned ashen, then she burst into tears. "Oh my God, it's not true, it can't be true," she sobbed. Then the sobs turned to hysteria.

"What's wrong, what can't be true?" asked Amelia. Leila was sobbing uncontrollably. She put her head in her hands as the letter fell to the floor. "I trusted him; he was my mentor and he did this to me," she yelled.

Amelia was shaken by this outburst, so she took Leila in her arms, not knowing what it was all about.

"Read the letter, Mother," she yelled.

Amelia picked up the letter and began reading and it

wasn't long before she understood what this outburst was all about. The letter asked for Leila to come to the solicitor's office, as Mr Letterman's estate was left to his two children, a son and a daughter, the daughter being named as Willow. Amelia's mind went back to her father and now this had happened to Leila, a man who was old enough to be her father. She thought all was forgotten of her own childhood, but no, it was still there as a reminder; it was as if it was never going to leave her, and now Leila was experiencing that same feeling.

Once Leila gathered her self-composure, she asked Amelia to look after Willow as she just had to get out, to leave the house and be on her own. She didn't want to look at her daughter. Was she always going to be a reminder of the man she trusted, the very man who stole her dignity and her virginity? As she thought back, she remembered on several occasions their paths had crossed and he had shown a vested interest in her baby, even to the point of asking what she had called her. No wonder, because he was her father.

Just the thought brought a rush of tears and she wanted to run away from it all, so picked up her pace and headed to God knows where. Her mind was in shut-down mode, so on she ran. It wasn't until she felt faint that she saw a seat in the park so sat down and let it all pour out. The hate had to be let go. It didn't change anything. She was the mother of his child, and it wasn't Willow's fault; she couldn't hate her because of what happened. How was she ever going to trust anyone again?

Amelia worried about Leila as she had been gone for

several hours. What would her reaction be towards Willow, who was the innocent party in all this? With this thought, she picked Willow up and cuddled her, telling her she was an angel lent to her and she loved her. Because she had been denied the pleasure of having any children of her own, she felt blessed having two girls to call her own, even though by law, they didn't rightfully belong to her. So many years had passed and Leila had never questioned her background, because all the love she needed was given to her by Amelia, who to her was her whole life. Amelia hoped this wouldn't have a bearing on her not wanting to meet someone and fall in love. She didn't want her to experience the heartache she had suffered, then stoop to stealing someone else's child to fulfil her own happiness.

While she was cuddling Willow and shedding her own tears, Amelia heard the door open and in walked Leila. How her heart ached to tell her about her own misery, but she couldn't, as it would open a can of worms. "I have been thinking, the last person I remember seeing that morning at the clubrooms was him, but honest to God, who would have believed a grown man would do such a terrible injustice to a teenage girl? Thank goodness I didn't live that experience, and all that was left for me to do was pick up the pieces. I can't believe Willow is a beneficiary to his will. I wonder how old the son is, as he will be her half-brother. I have never hated anyone in my life up until now, but I feel hatred towards him for his selfish behaviour, but then out of all this we have Willow. Come here, my darling," and with this the little girl ran to her mother. This was utter relief for Amelia as it could have ended a lot differently.

Today Amelia and Willow accompanied Leila to the solicitor's office. When they were asked in, the solicitor looked surprised; who was the beneficiary here he wondered. He addressed Amelia and began to explain the situation, but when he was told Willow was the beneficiary, he looked shocked. Amelia soon put him in the picture. "I am the mother; Leila is my daughter who was raped by this man and Willow is the outcome of this rape." The solicitor looked embarrassed; he needed time to take all this in, as he had no idea this was the situation.

"I don't understand, this little girl is so young. Mr Letterman was an older man, his son is twenty-six and here we have a toddler," he stammered.

"I told you what happened. He raped her while in a position of trust at the surf lifesaving club," shouted Amelia.

"I'm so sorry. I had no knowledge of this happening."

Silence reigned until he gathered his senses then he continued. "Mr Letterman owns a substantial piece of real estate, in fact a 10-acre farm on the outskirts of town. His son is in Vancouver studying criminal justice. I have spoken to him and he wants his half-sister to administer their father's affairs, as he has another year to complete his studies before he returns to Australia. What are we going to do now?"

Again, silence reigned. Amelia and Leila stared at each

other in bewilderment. Here was a dilemma, an estate without either of the beneficiaries able to run it.

"Leave it with me and I will contact his son and explain the situation. Just a thought, Leila, would you consider moving in and managing the property? I know this is not an ideal situation but give it some thought, and I will come back to you. If you want me to take you out to have a look, let me know." With this he stood up and shook Leila's hand and he apologised for the third time.

When they left his office, he sat down and wiped his brow with his handkerchief. He was shocked to think his friend had raped a young girl, in fact a teenager, while in a position of trust at the surf lifesaving club. Someone would have to know about this. It was not going to be ignored, and he would see that it was brought out in the open. He sat for a several minutes before ringing Vancouver with the terrible news.

Mr Letterman's son Mitchell was shocked at what he had been told of his father's appalling actions. To think his half-sister was only a toddler; his feelings turned towards the victim. He knew his father was a man about town, but for him to pick on a teenage girl was the pits. He wanted the solicitor to convey his condolences to Leila and he would be happy if she felt she *could* be the caretaker of the property until he returned. He would understand under the circumstances if she refused, and in fact he asked for her phone number so he could call her himself.

But first the solicitor would check to see if it was okay. What a day, one he would rather not have had! How was he going to handle his friend's betrayal, as he himself was a man of principles and high morals, so this situation could not go unaccounted for. A position of trust was just that, and if this was swept under the carpet then no one would know that an innocent person had suffered at the hands of this man. He felt he would not be doing justice to Leila or himself if it was not reported. His first contact would be the surf lifesaving club.

It wasn't long before the news circulated around the surf club. At first everyone was in denial: this was their mentor, they looked up to him. But as more details were released their estimations of him soon began to plummet. Especially when one of their fellow club members was the victim. Is that why Lee Lee left the team suddenly and never returned? No one understood why, but now it was out in the open. His saving grace was he was no longer around to take any punishment and his unsavoury memory would soon be forgotten. It didn't take long before the media jumped on the bandwagon ... here was a story worth getting hold of, which would gather momentum as well as sympathy. But someone was going to suffer.

The media made a beeline for the surf club to try to find out who the victim was, as they wanted her story ... what a windfall! All the members were asked to respect the victim and not to give out any information, but there was a whistle-blower in their midst. The next beeline was to Amelia's home where the doorbell started ringing. When she came to the door and saw the reporters, she told them to go away, to respect the victim not harass her, then she shut the door. But the doorbell rang until late at night and started again early in the morning. Leila was followed everywhere but refused to speak to any media. Amelia rang the police, and their intervention relieved some of the pressure off Leila. Once the story was out and the victim was unnamed, the media stopped harassing her, so life returned to near normal. But still people wanted to let Leila know how they felt, so the sympathy was endless.

This was when she decided she would contact the solicitor to ask him to take her to have a look at the property, so she could get away from it all. It was too much for her, as she had exams coming up and needed to be in a peaceful environment. Today was the day the solicitor was picking her up, a Saturday so there was no varsity and Amelia was taking Willow to Sea World for the afternoon. They drove in silence until they reached the property, which she noticed was all fenced and had a tree-lined driveway. As they entered, she saw a lovely modern house surrounded by lovely gardens.

The car stopped at the front entrance and before the solicitor alighted, he touched Leila on the arm. "On Mitchell's instructions I have had all Alister Letterman's personal items removed, his clothing, his footwear and his photographs, so there are no reminders of who once lived here. Just think of this as a house viewing." With this he climbed out of the car and came around and opened the door for her, then they walked towards the entrance. Before she entered, Leila asked, "Is there a Mrs Letterman?" He told her they had parted many years ago, in fact when Mitchell was still at school, but he didn't know where she was now. As he opened the door, she was a little hesitant; was this really where she wanted to be? Suddenly all the media hype and the jostling for a story came flooding back; yes, this had to be done. No ill feelings came to the fore as she walked around and no evidence of who had lived here was visible.

"Mitchell also asked for all the bedding, cushions and throws to be replaced so all the furnishing are new. He is hoping you will make this your home. He asked for your phone number, but I told him I would need your permission. I will leave you to walk around and I will go back and sit in the car."

Leila was happy for this time on her own as it gave her time to think about things and to get a feeling for the house. She could imagine Willow with a pet as there was plenty of ground for her to play. Perhaps it was time for her to have somewhere of her own to become more independent.

They drove back to Amelia's home and stopped outside. The solicitor could see that Leila was deep in thought so left it up to her to speak first.

"Thank you for taking me out there today. I need to think this over. I'll be back in touch when I have made a decision. If Mitchell wants to call me, that's fine." On these parting words she climbed out of the car and walked towards the house.

He watched her walk up the path and wondered whether she was interested in the property. He hoped so, as she certainly deserved some sort of recompense for all she had been through. He was bitterly disappointed with his friend. He knew he had had a roving eye, but a teenage girl, what on earth was he thinking? He was happy this would be the final dealings with him, as in his eyes he was nothing short of a monster.

A week passed, and many thoughts had been swirling around in Leila's head: should she, shouldn't she, was it right or not? Still she wasn't sure. The little anxiety about who the property belonged to would not leave her; was this always going to plague her?

Suddenly she was disturbed by a phone call. "Hello, Leila, this is Mitchell calling. I don't know what to say, other than apologise profusely for my father's behaviour. No words can explain how disappointed I feel. I am not at all like him, so please don't judge me by his actions. I knew he was no angel, but to stoop to the level he did makes this conversation feel uncomfortable.

"The solicitor told me you had been to view the property, and I was wondering what you have decided. Unfortunately, I cannot come back until the end of the year, as if I leave the country, my visa will be cancelled and I want to finish my study in forensics. In the end I would like to come back but that will depend on your decision. Don't think I am pressurising you, but your gut feeling will let you know what feels right. If it is not, then just let us know."

Leila was taken aback by this conversation, as Mitchell seemed a decent young man. He sounded remorseful for what had happened to her, although he was not responsible for his father's actions. She took a moment or two to gather her thoughts. "I have been thinking seriously about moving in, as it would allow me to escape the media attention, which is really bugging me. Also I have exams coming up so a peaceful place would be good for me."

With this he interrupted. "What media attention are you experiencing?"

Leila let him know that the story was out about his father and her as the victim, although her name was not publicised.

He was full of apologies. "How embarrassing for you. Try to be brave as it will pass, and in the meantime I will call you often and support you. I know the property is not encumbered with any debt but there will be rates and insurances to pay, so I will attend to that. I will give you a call in a couple of days to see what you have decided. Until then, take care."

Leila was a little more relaxed after this call, as she felt he was genuinely concerned for her. Perhaps she should think seriously about moving out to the farm. In the end the estate was to be shared between Mitchell and Willow, so yes, she had a vested interest in it. Now came the hardest part and that was to break the news to Amelia, who was not happy when she found out about the property. She didn't want to lose control of her two girls as they were her whole life. First, Leila would have to get her driver's licence so she could drive to varsity and then drop Willow off at Amelia's on the way. Tonight, she would have a serious talk with Amelia and tell her of her decision.

The talk didn't end well as Amelia was against Leila moving, as it meant she would lose some control over her life. Leila explained that it wouldn't happen until she got her driver's licence, but she and Willow would spend the weekends at the farm come back on Sunday night. "You will still have Willow during the week while I am at varsity, then you will have your weekends free. It is time you found someone as I have taken up years of your life, and now it's time for you."

This was not what Amelia wanted to hear. She certainly didn't want a man in her life; she just wanted her two girls. Not that Leila knew of Amelia's tragic life as a young girl. She naturally thought it was time for her to find male company.

As Amelia dropped Leila and Willow off at the farm she felt a piece of her life had ended. She felt alone and sad; now it would just be her on her own at the weekends. She had not seen this day ever happening. It was never meant to be like this in her ideal world. She suddenly had a thought. 'What would happen if something happened to me, how would Leila know her roots?' This was a worry? Perhaps she should prepare a statement that would reveal all. But that was years away; she would wait for another few years.

It was Saturday night and she was watching television, when all of a sudden she flicked on to a channel that was talking about a prominent Gold Coast surf lifesaver who had taken advantage of a teenage lifesaver who he was mentoring. "The man was old enough to be her father and sadly a baby had been born from this liaison. Because he was in a position of trust, this had to be brought out in the open, to make people aware that their daughters were not safe even in a club, where trust was paramount. This case has just been brought to our attention as the perpetrator had passed away and the victim didn't know who raped her as she was drugged. It wasn't until his will was read that the truth was revealed, much to the horror of the victim. All names have been withheld, but this case needs to be publicised because of the trauma the victim suffered…"

Amelia was shocked. Who the hell released this information, and where else was it going to be aired?

After tonight's discussion on the photo Lily had shown the family, it was agreed by all that they must find out more about this girl, but where would they start? Lily decided to get the ball rolling by approaching a forensic artist to do an age-progression image of Leila, and Kennedy would take the photo to a notable photographer, to take out everything on the photo, just leaving the young lady and the little girl.

Now it was time for Kennedy to leave as this night the boys were meeting at Lincoln's home. Both Kennedy and Reece knew what to expect as Lincoln greeted them at the door. Had they mixed with anyone who had Covid? Were they clear of flus and colds? This was a routine check for anyone who visited him. He was paranoid about Covid; as yet he hadn't had it and certainly didn't want it, so scrutiny was paramount! All his shopping was done online and delivered to his door, as now he had confined himself to his own property and most of that time was spent indoors. He hadn't lost contact with his friends; they Zoom talked and interacted through virtual reality. The virtual reality of today would not meet tomorrow's increasing demands, because people wanted faster, smother and lifelike scenarios. But with this came the problem of greater demands on processing speed, memory and rendering time. This was an area which needed to be addressed before virtual reality could advance to its full potential. Lincoln spoke to the lads on these facts.

Kennedy apologised for Harrison's no-show, as he had an important night lecture he had to attend, but he did give him some facts to read out. 'In the virtual reality world at this time, more than half of the VR market is gaming based, next is the medical industry, then education, followed by various other workplaces.'

"So yes, there is definitely money to be made in the gaming industry, but how do we go about it?" Kennedy asked. Being the technology nerd this was an easy decision for Lincoln. His company along with his expertise were developing a new gaming strategy that was going to be launched at the end of the year and would need shareholders. He told his company not to advertise as he had shareholders waiting to invest. He himself would be a big investor along with Kennedy and Reece. He was hoping they could raise the money needed to become the sole shareholders outside of the company, as he could see a fortune waiting to be made. So why not them?

Kennedy and Lincoln still had most of their cryptocurrency fortune in their wallet, but for Reece it was a different matter. He had withdrawn his share to put into buying a hotel with Natalia. This was followed by the partnership break-up, so his fortune was halved. Sadly, out of his crypto fortune Lily received very little. If it wasn't for Kennedy helping her to purchase a share in the law firm, she wouldn't be the wealthy lady she was today. She had insisted on paying Kennedy back, much to his disappointment, but that was her independent streak! This left Reece with a shortfall compared to his friend's wealth, but with true friendships, they were not about to forget that if not for his inheritance, they would not be where they were today.

Lily had an appointment with a forensic artist to talk about age progression. He told her he would prefer to come to her home and meet the family, which she thought was strange. She arranged a time and date for this to happen and for the whole family including Reece to be there as he was Leila's biological father.

That evening they all gathered around the table waiting in anticipation to see if he could help them find their missing daughter. First, he asked for a photo of Leila, one as near as possible to her disappearance date, as well as one of the mother and father and any siblings. Mackenzie rushed away to her bedroom to get a photo of herself, but little did she know this was about to open a can of worms! Lily and Kennedy had not told the twins he was their biological father, not Reece as they had believed. Tonight, this was all going to change. "Here is my photo. In fact you are in it, Harrison, so you don't need a photo," she offered. Lily had put off explaining the situation to the twins, as she felt they had suffered enough with the loss of their sister. Besides, it didn't seem important any more.

"Why do you need a photo of siblings?" she asked. The artist explained that if he could see how they had aged, then that was a significant help. Now the truth had to come out, but how would she start? Kennedy came to her rescue as always, as he felt a load had been put on Lily. "What if the siblings had a different father, does that change your findings?" he asked.

"What do you mean by asking that?" said Mackenzie.

"I'm sorry you must find out the truth tonight. Leila is Reece's daughter and you and Harrison are my biological children. We haven't told you before now, as we have all been through a lot as a family. Does it worry you?" he asked.

The twins were shocked, especially to find out Leila was their half-sister rather than a full sister. Harrison sat quietly not saying a word, but Mackenzie couldn't hold her peace, "Why didn't you tell us before now? Not that it really matters, as to us Leila is our sister regardless, isn't she Harrison?" He nodded in response. "But this is not the end," she warned.

Now it was time for the forensic artist to tell them of the process. "We use specialised software to create a digital model of the child's face, then add age-related changes, including changes to the skull and features such as nose, ears and mouth. The image is then fine-tuned and carefully reviewed and adjusted to ensure it is as accurate as possible. That is why we ask for photos of the parents as well as the siblings. In your case, this is not the norm, but we will take the photo of the twins, in case we feel it will help us. Age progression is not an exact science, but it has proven to be an effective tool in locating missing children. Leave this with me and I will get back to you as soon as it has been processed."

Lily thanked him for coming as she let him out. Now they had to face a barrage of questions from the twins.

Two weeks later the forensic artist dropped the age-progression images into Lily's chambers. As she studied them, she felt overwhelmed as this image was a close match to the girl in Reece's photo. She felt the trauma this girl had gone through; she was just a teenager who had become a mother. Tears trickled down her cheeks as she thought of Leila. This couldn't possibly be her, as she was just a child who had her whole life ahead of her. Lily wiped away her tears then picked up her briefcase and put the closed sign on the door of her chambers and drove home.

On arriving home, she found the twins immersed in their computers. Harrison's nose was in the gaming sector and Mackenzie was shopping for more clothes for her avatar. Lily asked them to come to the table as she had the images from the forensic artist. As she lay the images out, Mackenzie was the first to comment, "Oh my God, that looks like the girl in the photo. Could she be our Leila? But why would she be living in Australia?" The next comment came from Harrison, "Why wouldn't she be living over there? Remember someone stole her. The New Zealand police couldn't find her, so it is common sense to think someone took her out of the country, but you are right, it does look like the girl in the photo. If that is Leila, then I'm an uncle," he said proudly.

Lily and Mackenzie dismissed Harrison's comment, as they were thinking of the trauma this person had suffered, but perhaps a male would not understand as they didn't have maternal feelings.

Lily invited Reece around so she and Kennedy could go over the artist's images with him. He was blown away as he compared the photo to the images, as he also saw a likeness to Leila. He looked at Lily and tears came from nowhere, "To think I met her and didn't even know my own daughter, our child Lily and I didn't even recognise her," he sobbed. Lily went to Reece and hugged him. He clung to her as he needed to feel the comfort of a loved one.

"You are our lead on this Reece. Tell us what you remember of your chance meeting with this young lady. We need every clue you can give us," said Lily.

He took stock of himself; he had to concentrate and try to recall what conversation had taken place. He remembered she took her little girl to the theme park every Saturday as she had no uni classes at the weekend, and that she lived close to Sea World. He told them all he knew, then he remembered that the girl from the photo shop had called her Lee Lee. The rest of the conversation he wished he could forget but elected to tell them.

"She never went back to the surf lifesaving club and no one knew why, until they heard something terrible had happened to her. Oh, she also said she was studying law as she wanted to protect vulnerable young girls from male predators. I wonder if she was referring to her own situation. Perhaps that's what the girl from the photo shop meant? We must find her Lily; she was our baby and we loved her."

Kennedy added: "If only we knew how to get in touch with Amelia. Damn her for not leaving her phone number with us, as we can't contact her. I wonder if they are still at Forster-Tuncurry where her man was working. It would be a guessing game to try and find her. We can't go down that avenue, that door is closed."

Silence reigned as their minds went back to the girl in the photo. "I am thinking I will go back to the Gold Coast and try and find her, or even speak to the girl in the photo shop. Surely I can get a lead," said Reece.

"If you find her, Reece, call me. I am in the middle of an important civil case at the moment, but our daughter comes first," replied Lily.

But Reece had just taken his holidays so he would have to check with his boss to see if he could get another week off his annual leave. Then he would have to book a flight, so it wasn't going to happen for a couple of weeks.

Everyone was stirred up as they were convinced the girl in the photo was Leila. Nothing much was mentioned about the little girl who was with her as it was incomprehensible to think Leila had a child as she was so young.

"What if Leila is not her mother? Perhaps we are chasing a rainbow as there must be people who have doubles. We must be sure before we act," remarked Mackenzie.

Lily agreed, and she knew that if parenthood met with denial, there was always a DNA test.

Back in Australia

A month had passed since their last family meeting, as it had taken this long for Reece to arrange another week away from the hotel and to finalise his flight plans. Today was Friday and he had flown into Coolangatta from Queenstown then caught a shuttle from the airport to the Marina Mirage where he had stayed on his last visit. It was 2.30, he felt restless so decided to walk up to the photo shop to begin his search, as he couldn't wait until tomorrow, as he felt it was wasted time.

At the shop he was surprised as there was a new face behind the counter. "Excuse me, last time I was here there was a young lady who served me. Is she still working here?" asked Reece. The lady told him the previous assistant had gone to Melbourne to work and she herself had just arrived on the Gold Coast from Sydney.

"How can I help you?" she asked.

He felt deflated, as she would not be able to give him the information he sought. He thanked her and left the shop to begin his walk back to the resort, but not without shedding tears on the way. He was not expecting to feel so disappointed, as he was quite upbeat when he started off on his walk, thinking he would have some good news to send home, but this was not to be. He had dinner then went straight to bed and before long he was sound asleep.

On waking in the morning, he noticed his phone was flickering as there was a message for him. It was from Lily wanting to know if he had any news. He didn't want to talk to her so sent a text telling her what had transpired yesterday. Sadly there wasn't much joy to relay, but he would call her tonight.

Hopefully today was going to be a turning point, so off he set, to walk to Sea World. He even had a spring in his step because he was thinking positively. Being Saturday, the crowds were lining up at the gates as everyone wanted to be first through, so in the line he waited to purchase his pass. Once through, he stopped to think where he would begin, as it was too early to buy lunch, so he wandered around aimlessly hoping to see the young lady and the child. He was there for one reason only, so he was not much interested in the rides or the performances. Reece started at one end of the park and zigzagged through the crowds, peering in all the little nooks and crannies that housed all sorts of craft products, as well as food stalls. But his searching was fruitless, and when food got the better of him, he bought a hot-dog and chips and headed to the park area, where crowds had gathered with the same intention as himself. Here he looked over, through and around the people but still luck eluded him; she was nowhere to be seen.

He decided to stand at the entrance of the theme park in case he might catch sight of her as she came through the gates. Two hours passed and still no sign. He knew she said she came every Saturday as she had no varsity, so why wasn't she here? His eye was taken by all the Arab people dressed in their white gowns. Were they residents or visitors he wondered. When there was a lull at one of the gates, he asked a staff member. He told Reece that it was Arab season as they had come to Australia to escape the sweltering 45-degree heat back in their own country. Well, that was one bit of useful information he had received today!

The staff member had seen him waiting at the gates so asked him why he was there, so Reece told him he was waiting for someone. "Give me a name and I will call out over the speaker." What could Reece say? He didn't have a name, then he remembered her nickname. He told the staff member all he had was Lee Lee but no surname.

"I'll give it a go, but it will be a long shot," he said. Within minutes a message rang out over the loudspeaker system, "If you are here Lee Lee, please come to entrance gate number one."

Reece thanked him and patiently waited … and waited … and waited. "Looks like you are out of luck today mate," yelled the staff member. Reece was not about to give up as there were still two hours left until the gates shut. But, again, luck was not with him, as at 5.30 it was announced the gates would be shutting at 6 o'clock. Another unsuccessful day; was she not meant to be found? Everything seemed to be working against him.

Back in his hotel suite a despondent Reece called Lily, "Hi Lily, I have had a terrible day as she didn't turn up at Sea World. I don't know where to turn to next." Lily reminded him about the surf lifesaving club: perhaps someone there might be able to help. Or perhaps if he waited outside the university, he may just find her there during the week. He ended the call by telling Lily he missed her. This she took with a grain of salt, but for Reece it had much more meaning; it came from his heart.

This morning being Sunday, Reece was up early and went to the dining room for breakfast, as he had decided to go to the surf lifesaving club to see if someone might talk to him about Lee Lee. It was a lovely warm morning and as he neared the surf club, he could see all the young lifesavers going through their drill. It was only a fifteen-minute walk from the Resort and in the distance, he could see the colourful boatsheds gleaming in the sun, so he reached for his camera and took a photo. He decided to get a closer shot after he had been to the clubhouse. He watched the boys and girls being put through a rigorous workout as they had to be fit to be a lifesaver. Reece made his way up to where the older members were gathering and mingled with them, hoping to find someone he could talk to. One of the members had noticed him, so approached and asked if he could help. Reece was not sure if he should ask straight out about Lee Lee or just start with general conversation. He decided the latter would be best, so said how great it was to see the youngsters taking part with so much enthusiasm in their drill. Once the pleasantries were over Reece felt now was the time to ask questions.

"Do you know of a young lady called Lee Lee who used to be a lifesaver here at this club?" Suddenly the tone of the conversation changed. "Are you a reporter?" asked the man. Reece assured him he had a genuine interest in this young lady as he had met her and her daughter when he last came to Australia, and he wanted to make contact with her again. The man asked him to come outside so they could talk in private.

"We have been told not to discuss Lee Lee's business, as it brought negative publicity to our surf club. But obviously you know her, so I will tell you what happened. Her then mentor drugged her and took her to a boatshed and raped her. When she woke, she didn't know where she was, or what had happened to her. No one knew about this as she never pressed charges. It wasn't until a year or so later when her mentor died and left his estate to a son and daughter that Lee Lee's daughter was named as a beneficiary to his estate. This was when she found out he was the rapist."

Reece was stunned by this revelation. If this was his Leila, no, this could not have happened to her surely? He gathered his thoughts and asked, "She told me she lived near the theme park. Do you know her address?" The man would not give out any personal information as the surf club members had been forbidden to make Lee Lee's life any more complicated, as she had been hounded by reporters for months. After hearing this, Reece turned away and tears came to his eyes and trickled down his cheeks as he thought of what she had gone through. Even if it wasn't Leila, he would have felt the same for any young girl who had become a victim of rape. He thanked the man for giving out the information he asked for, as now he had a first-hand insight into what this girl had gone through. Deep down he hoped this wasn't their Leila as he knew it would break Lily's heart, as it did his.

The colourful boatsheds had suddenly lost their shine, now that Reece knew this was the place where all had taken place, so he decided to make the one photo he had taken earlier the one and only. It was a shame, as they looked so picturesque shining in the sun. He wondered how such a beautiful backdrop hid such dark secrets when they could have brought happiness to many.

On this note, he made his way back to his accommodation in a solemn mood. The first thing he did when he entered his suite was go to his suitcase and take out the photo. His heart was heavy as he went over all he had been told today and was thankful the man from the surf club took him aside and explained everything, but that's where it started and ended! He was still no closer to finding Leila. Reece called Lily and told her about the day's findings, which brought gasps from her end, even sobs as she learnt what had happened.

"Tomorrow I'm going to go door knocking and show people the photo and ask as many questions as I can, in the hope of finding Lee Lee."

Reece was up bright and early this morning, he was on

a mission as he had worked out a strategy, so was keen to put it into practice. As he had visited the theme park several times, he knew what streets ran parallel to Seaworld Drive. He hadn't done door knocking before so this was a whole new experience.

After several hours, still no luck came his way, and residents weren't very helpful as many didn't even know their neighbours, probably because most properties had high fences and security gates. With one more house to go Reece was feeling weary but would not give in, he had to see this street completed, so he could start a new one tomorrow. He walked up the path and rang the doorbell. When the door opened, he got the shock of his life. There stood Amelia.

"Good God, what are you doing here?" he asked. Poor Amelia, she was just as surprised as Reece, and then panic took over. She had to think quick as a nightmare was unfolding before her, and she was lost for words.

"We thought you were still on the road; do you live here?" he asked.

She couldn't invite Reece in as there were photos of Leila and Willow all around the home. "Actually, you have come at a bad time as my partner is very sick with Covid and I am just getting over it. We were here house-sitting for friends when we got sick, so they let us have their home until we get better. I'm sorry I can't invite you in. What brings you to Surfers and where are you staying?" she asked.

Reece explained he was just up the street at the Marina

Mirage. "I am here to try and find Leila, I had a lead when I was here a while back, but luck is not with me this time."

"What do you mean? Did you actually see her?" asked Amelia.

Reece explained about meeting a young lady and her daughter at the theme park and she said she lived near, so he was trying to find out where she lives. "She looked so much like we presumed Leila to be. Lily asked a forensic artist to draw an ageing picture of Leila and it is very similar to the young lady I met. She actually appeared in a photo I took of the dolphins. She was in the second row so we had it blown up and the animals removed."

Amelia suddenly thought that he must be who Leila talked to at the theme park one day. She was getting fidgety as Willow was due to wake from her afternoon sleep, so she told Reece her partner was calling so she had to go. "I will come and see you tomorrow night, perhaps we could have a drink together?" she suggested, thinking she had to keep Reece from visiting her again. This was a close shave, which worried her; he was the last person she expected to see. As she closed the door, she said goodbye, which left him standing and feeling a little bewildered. Was this just pure luck that he found Amelia? Fancy her house-sitting right here at this time. He forgot to ask her how long she would be there, but perhaps he could ask when they met again. On reflection, the day wasn't a complete disaster as he had met up with his half-sister.

Reece was on the phone to Lily to let her know what had happened. There was no news on Leila, but he had stumbled across Amelia who was house-sitting for a friend. "Did she invite you in?" Lily asked. Reece told her the conversation was held at the front door as her partner was sick with Covid.

"I wonder if she can help us find Leila. How long is she staying on the Gold Coast?" quizzed Lily. Reece told her he would find out when they next met. Tomorrow he would get another early start as there were three more streets to canvass, and surely somebody would recognise the girl in the photo. But to stumble on Amelia, what a surprise. Perhaps he could even meet her man friend, then he could tell Kennedy what he thought of him, as he was worried Amelia's money was the drawcard.

Today started much like yesterday, and no one seemed to recall seeing the young lady in the photo. Was this another wasted day? Reece just needed a lucky break; surely someone could help? He saw a couple of teenage girls in lifesaving T-shirts so he called out to them.

"I was wondering if you know this girl in the photo. Her name is Lee Lee and she lives close to Sea World." He showed the girls the photo and they said yes, she lived in that street in the big house with her mother, but she has shifted now. At last, a break. "Do you mean that street?" asked Reece as he pointed to the one Amelia lived in. "Yes, that's the one, the big house." Reece scratched his head, but that was the house where Amelia was staying. "Are you sure?" he asked. The girls assured him that was where she lived.

This sent him into a quandary. Should he keep searching or would he go back to where Amelia was staying and ask if her friend had a daughter? Yes, that's what he would do. As he made his way up the path, unbeknown to him Amelia had spotted him so rushed and locked the front door and crept up to Willow's bedroom so she wouldn't be seen. She heard him knocking at the door and he didn't give up easily, but in the end he left. Reece thought she must have gone out as no one answered the door. Just when he thought he had a lead … again nothing eventuated. He consoled himself with the thought they were meeting tonight for a drink so he would ask her then.

Reece had a shower and changed, so he would feel fresh when he met with Amelia. He made his way to the bar and didn't have to wait long before she arrived. "Hi Reece," she greeted him. She had prepared herself mentally for a barrage of questions.

"How's your man?" he asked. She told him he was sick and still in bed.

"How long are you staying at your friends' place?"

Amelia said she didn't know as it depended on her partner's health.

"Does your friend have a daughter?" was the next question. This caught Amelia off guard. Why was he asking this, what was this leading to? Her heart began racing and before she had time to think of an answer, Reece asked what age the daughter was. This gave Amelia a clue, as he obviously knew something. Thank goodness she had hesitated before answering. "I think she is in her late teens or even perhaps twenty. I haven't seen her this visit. Why do you ask?"

Reece told her he had spoken with a couple of young

girls and shown them the photo and they said she lived at this address and her name was Lee Lee. "Has your friend spoken to you and told you what had happened to her daughter?" Again, Amelia was caught off guard. What the hell did he know, what was he going to come out with next, where was this leading? She felt trapped. She was not expecting these questions. How much did he really know?

"She told me there was an incident at the surf club and now her daughter was living with a friend. I really don't know much more as we are still living at Forster-Tuncurry and are just house-sitting."

Reece asked how long she had known her friend. She had to think as she didn't want to be caught out so had to cover her steps. "Oh, we only met a couple of years back when she came to stay at the resort we are working at. We just seemed to click and had some wild nights together. I don't know much about her life really, as we never got around to discussing our pasts, so I can't tell you much more."

Reece realised he wasn't going to get much more on her friend. "Will you give me her name and phone number?" Amelia told him to come around tomorrow and she would give him the information he wanted. Now the questions came from Amelia as she wanted to know all that was happening back in New Zealand, so Reece was busy filling her in.

"Write your phone number with your friends so we can contact you more often," he requested. It didn't take long for the night to slip by as Amelia was worried about her partner, so they said their goodbyes, until tomorrow.

Reece did a lot of thinking about his meeting with Amelia. He wasn't quite sure if she was trying to avoid his questions as she dithered a lot before finally answering. He felt he was making inroads and tomorrow this could be where it all fell into place. In the morning he would go to Amelia's friend's house and collect all the information he needed, phone numbers and names, then it would be just a matter of time.

Reece marched up the path to the house feeling pleased with himself. After last night's conversation he was keen to get all the details promised to him. He knocked on the door and waited … and waited … and waited, but no one answered. He tried many times with the same result. Perhaps her partner needed hospital treatment; he would come back later. It was now dusk and this was the fifth time Reece had made the journey to where Amelia was house-sitting, with the same result: no answer. He would come back tomorrow.

The next day was no different to the day before: no one was home. Reece saw a neighbour in her garden so approached her. "Excuse me, is everything all right at that house? I had arranged to meet Amelia, but there has been no answer. I was wondering if her partner was okay." The lady looked at Reece in astonishment. "Amelia lives on her own. She doesn't have a partner; she looks after a little girl each day."

"Are you sure?" asked Reece. "She told me she was house-sitting for a friend."

The neighbour told Reece she had lived there for many years. He stood and scratched his head. What was going on? Why would she lie to him? He felt stupid so thanked the lady and left. Tomorrow was his last day in Australia, so he had to catch up with Amelia before he left and find out why she had lied.

He arrived back at the resort in a fluster. He had to talk to Lily. He called her and told her the untruths he had been fed by Amelia and was at a loss to understand why. He only had tomorrow to catch up with her; it was his last chance before he returned home. Lily was just as upset as Reece on hearing what had happened. Why would she lie? Perhaps her relationship had floundered, and she didn't want them to know.

This was Reece's fourth trip back to Amelia's home today and still no one was answering the door. As it was just on dusk, he decided to be nosey so walked around the house and peered in the windows on the lower floor, but nothing seemed amiss. He did notice the neighbour on the other side watching him, making him feel uncomfortable, so he went back to the front door and knocked again, but still no joy.

Reece resigned himself to the fact that this was the end of his meetings with Amelia. He lay on his bed and tried to put it all together. The two young girls told him Lee Lee lived at the same address as Amelia. What was the tie-up? Why had she said they were still working at Forster-Tuncurry and were just house-sitting? All he could think of was the relationship had gone sour many years ago and she couldn't bring herself to tell them the truth, as they were sceptical about the relationship at the start. Had he taken so much of her fortune that she was reduced to child-minding during the day? Reece was disappointed in himself as now he was still at a loss as to where Lee Lee fitted into the picture. In the morning before he caught the bus to the airport, he would leave a letter in Amelia's letterbox asking her to call him in New Zealand as he needed some answers.

A shocking revelation

Lily, Kennedy and the twins were sitting around the table listening to Reece relaying his uneventful experience in Australia. Kennedy listened with intent and was shocked to think Amelia had fed him so many lies. He had placed faith in her and hoped they would remain a family as it took years for them to find each other, but now he felt they were drifting apart. "Do you think her partner may have taken her to the cleaners over money?" he asked. Reece told them she lived in a very expensive home but did wonder why she was child-minding. Perhaps he had taken half her fortune. All they could do now was wait to hear from her.

The days passed by and no contact was made. Tonight, while Lily and her family were watching TV a 'Breaking news story' was flashing. "A burglary gone wrong on the Gold Coast of Australia had resulted in two bodies being discovered. The police weren't releasing any more details until the bodies were identified."

Immediately Lily called Reece to see if he had seen the news, as he had just come back from there. The rest of the day went by and in the late news that night, more details were released on the murder. The victims had been identified as a female and a child. Now it was Reece who contacted Lily. "As soon as I heard this, I got goosebumps. Why am I feeling like this, Lily?" he asked.

She consoled him by saying it was a dreadful thing to have happened and many other people would be experiencing the same feelings.

In the morning more details were released. It looked like the burglar was disturbed as it was a daylight robbery. The female was child-minding her granddaughter, and this grizzly scene was discovered by the child's mother when she finished varsity and went to collect her daughter. She is now in hospital recovering from shock. No more news would be released until the next of kin were notified. Reece was straight on the phone to Lily. "Oh Lily, I'm worried. Lee Lee is at varsity. I hope that is not her daughter that has been murdered." He was frantic, so Lily told him to come around and they would talk.

Amelia's worst fears

Amelia was shocked when Reece turned up at her home, as she was not expecting it. Any visitors from New Zealand spelled disaster; would her life be exposed, and what would they think when the truth was out? Meeting him for a drink was risky, in fact on the side of dangerous. He'd asked so many questions for which she was unprepared, giving her the feeling he knew something. No way was she going to keep her appointment with Reece, because she wasn't going to give out information that would expose her little secret. She rang Leila and asked if she could come and stay for a couple of days and she would look after Willow in her own surroundings. Although this was out of character for Amelia to suggest this, Leila was quite happy as it just meant she didn't have to deviate on her way to varsity.

She had settled in at her new address, and the quietness she treasured, after all the publicity over her departure from the surf club. Although it had not all gone away the press had stopped harassing her, and now it was just the stares she received from people that knew what had happened. Most the people at varsity had heard through the grapevine so it was still a topic of conversation. Leila was surprised how well she had settled in; she had experienced no bad vibes or reminders of the past, so this allowed her to enjoy the quietness of the countryside. She enjoyed being independent; it gave her time to grow within herself. She had to think ahead and plan things, instead of having everything done for her. Amelia had spoilt her, so now it was time to stand on her own two feet, much to Amelia's disappointment. She wanted to be Leila's and Willow's forever mother but now that privilege was slowly being taken from her. She found the nights and weekends boring. But she was prompted to put together a letter to her solicitor for Leila, so she knew her roots if anything happened to her. She also left a letter to be sent to Kennedy, Reece and Lily on her death, explaining why she stole their daughter and the joy it brought to her life.

Mitchell had arranged a gardener to look after the property through his solicitor, so the lawns were kept tidy. He had spoken to Leila several times and a friendship was being formed, so she was looking forward to meeting him. It was only a couple more weeks before he returned from Canada. They hadn't discussed where he was going to live, but that would come later. He often enquired about Willow, which Leila thought was nice. How ironic to think his half-sister was twenty-six years younger than him and she, her mother, was also younger. To begin with, Mitchell was appalled at the age difference, although the more he had to do with Leila the less horrific it became. But he would never forgive his father for the grave injustice he had caused, especially while being in a position of trust.

Now that Amelia knew Reece had flown back to New Zealand, she returned to her home and the arrangements with Willow continued. She found his letter in her post box, read it then put it away with her personal papers for the time being, as she wasn't ready to deal with it. She heard Willow calling to her, so she went and picked her up, as her afternoon nap had ended. Amelia loved this little girl as she had not experienced a child this young, as Leila at this age belonged to Lily and Reece. These moments were special, as she loved the closeness of cuddling Willow. It caused her heart to sing; was this because she couldn't remember having these feelings when she was little? Her childhood memories were not pleasant and they grew worse as she got older. She felt she had given Leila and Willow a sense of security, a privilege that was taken away from her.

Amelia did not get to know her neighbours apart from saying hello to them. This was by choice, as the fewer people she knew the easier it was on her. She wished for nothing else other than to share her love, not with a male, but with her two girls. She was fortunate she had been left a legacy from her father, as this allowed her to be a full-time mother to Leila.

As she was dressing Willow, who was sitting on her

knee, she heard the front door slam shut. She waited and it was only when she looked up that she saw two balaclava-clad men standing beside her. She screamed in fright, and reached over and snatched the balaclava from one of the intruders. Now he was exposed.

"You have to get rid of her, she knows your face."

The other guy tried to take the child from her, but Amelia clung to Willow who had started crying. The next thing she saw was a gun pointing at her, then bang, she felt a hot rush of blood coming from her chest. Then came the second shot and they both fell to the floor. One of the men walked over and moved the bodies to make sure no one was alive to tell the story.

"Hurry! Let's see what we can find. You go upstairs and I'll search down here." The two intruders ransacked the home and took anything that looked valuable. "I've got the car keys and I found a satchel in the bottom drawer which is stuffed with money. Let's go," one yelled. They carried their loot down the hallway through the end passage door leading to the garage, unlocked the car and threw everything in. As they started the car, they pulled off their balaclavas. Next, they tried to find the device that opened the garage door without success, so one of the robbers jumped out and pushed the button on the garage wall, releasing the door. In an instant they left the property and headed north.

Varsity had finished for the day and Leila was on her way to pick up Willow. As she pulled up the driveway, she noticed the garage door was open but there was no car. "That's strange," she said to herself. Instead of going to the front door, Leila opted to go through the garage. As she was walking past the bedrooms she noticed clothes everywhere, then a sudden shiver ran down her spine. As she entered the dining room, she let out a blood-curling scream. There on the floor lay Amelia and Willow. She bent down only to see blood oozing out from where they lay. Again, she screamed then fell to the floor. Fortunately, the neighbour was in her garden and heard the scream so came over to see what was wrong, as she had seen Leila's car arrive a few minutes earlier. What confronted her was a horror crime scene. She ran to Leila and tried to wake her, but she was out cold. She rummaged through Leila's bag and found a cell phone and rang 000. She asked for the police and an ambulance.

The neighbour sat and held Leila's hand until someone arrived. The police were first to arrive and were shocked to see three bodies on the floor. The neighbour said Leila had just arrived and must have gone into shock when she saw the bodies. Next came the ambulance, but there was only one person to take away. The ambulance officers brought in a stretcher and lifted Leila onto it, as the police wanted her away from the scene. Once safely in the vehicle, one of the medics ran back into the home to hear what the police had to say about the remaining two people. He knew by the amount of blood on the carpet that there were no survivors, and this was confirmed by police.

The neighbour explained the family ties: there was a grandmother, a granddaughter and the person in the ambulance was the little girl's mother. The police thanked the neighbour and asked her to leave. If they had any more questions, they would come back to her. This property was now a murder scene, so it had to be cordoned off, to stop anyone coming anywhere near the home. The police were horrified. Here lay two innocent people in their own home, but a child, who would be so callous? As they moved through the property, they knew this was a burglary gone wrong. More police cars had arrived and this drew a lot of bystanders, all wondering what had happened. When the news got out about two murdered subjects inside, flowers started arriving.

Next on the scene was a forensic scientist who was trying to work out exactly what had happened. He could see gunshot wounds in the chest of the grandmother, but what of the child? As they moved her, they saw two wounds in her abdomen, so the bullets fired must have penetrated through the child into the grandmother. This pointed to the child having been sitting on her grandmother's knee when this horrific shooting occurred. Some of the police had tears in their eyes, as here were two innocent people cut down by a madman or madmen for no good reason ... other than to steal.

Meanwhile Leila was in hospital in a room of her own and with her was a nurse and a policewoman as she was not to be left on her own. No one knew if there were any other family members to be notified; it was still a mystery. What had Leila taken in, would she remember, or would her mind have blanked it all out? Perhaps the shock wiped everything completely. Only time would tell. The police needed to know more about the family: was there a reason, were they a target?

Back at the home the police had looked around trying to put things together. Going by the photos on the wall, there seemed to be only three members of this family. There were no men sighted in any photos. A policeman was sent next door to the neighbour, to find out what make of car had been taken from the garage. She told him the car was a sporty red Ferrari. She had seen it drive out an hour earlier, but took no notice of who was driving, or how many people were in the car. They had to get the details to the station so an alert could go out. He then asked about the family but was told they kept to themselves, so she couldn't tell them much more. She said the daughter and her daughter had lived at the house until several months ago, then they moved out to the countryside. The policeman thanked her and said he may have to come back another time, for more information if needed. He went back to his colleagues and passed the information on to them. The home, which was now a crime scene, would be under police surveillance 24/7. The bodies would stay where they lay, until further instructions were issued.

Two days had passed and Leila was still in shock; she had not yet woken. The doctor whose care she was in worried that perhaps if she remembered what had happened, she would never wake up. If there was no improvement by tomorrow, he would have to make some decisions.

When the solicitor who was handling the estate for

Mitchell and Willow heard through a police friend what had happened, he was devastated. How much more could Leila take, as if she hadn't had enough to deal with already. He drove to the hospital but was not allowed to see her. The nurse asked him to come to her office, as the policewoman wanted to speak with anyone connected to this family, so she then went to fetch her. Tears were rolling down the solicitor's face as he thought back to the reading of the will, when he had met the three of them in his office. Suddenly his phone went. "Hi, Mitchell here, I'm trying to contact Leila, she was meant to pick me up at the airport."

What could he say? There was no way he could tell him what had happened over the phone. "Wait there. I will come and pick you up now," he said.

"Is something wrong" Mitchell asked. The solicitor told him he would put him in the picture when they met. He couldn't afford to wait for the policewoman. He had to go, so that's what he did. When she did arrive no one was there, so she called for the nurse who was surprised he had gone, especially when he was to be questioned by the police. "Something urgent must have come up as he seemed keen to want to help," replied the nurse. Momentarily the policewoman was upset, as so far no one was able to throw any light on this family, so the case was at a standstill.

The solicitor drove to the airport and managed to find a park in the 'Pick-up' bay. He didn't know who he was looking for, as Mitchell was only a lad when he last saw him. There were several men standing waiting to be picked up, so he called out, "Mitchell," and a young man came over to him. He would never have picked him as he had grown up to be a fine young specimen. But if he had looked at the amount of luggage, that would have been a giveaway.

"Welcome home, Mitchell, are you bringing the whole of Canada back?" he asked.

Mitchell told him he had presents for Willow and Leila. They loaded the boot with the bags, then got into the car. Before he drove off, he told Mitchell he had some sad news for him and proceeded to tell him what had happened. He was shocked and put his head in his hands to hide the tears.

"Where is Leila now?" he asked. When he was told she was in hospital he asked the solicitor to take him there.

"No one is allowed to see her as she is still in shock."

"It doesn't matter. I will wait there. She needs someone to be there for her when she wakes," said Mitchell. The solicitor asked what he would to do with his luggage.

"Please take it to Leila's home and I will pick it up there, when I am sorted."

Mitchell was dropped off at the hospital. The solicitor asked him to apologise to the police for his hasty departure. He spoke with a nurse and said he was a friend of Leila's. She asked if she had any family and he said no. On hearing this she told him to come and sit at her bedside. He didn't tell the full story of how they became friends, as that was a private matter. He looked at Leila. This was his first sighting of her and he liked what he saw; she was a pleasant-looking young lady. Then suddenly a sobering thought shot threw his mind: here lay the victim his father had raped. He was overcome with a feeling of disgust. She was so young and was preyed upon by an older man, his father. What the hell was he thinking? With these thoughts Mitchell was pleased his father had passed away, otherwise he would have knocked him to the ground. He still felt the guilt that was his fathers. Would it ever go away?

He was disturbed by the door opening and in walked the policewoman. They greeted each other and Mitchell apologised for the solicitor's unexplained departure and told her why. So perhaps at last she could get some information, as up until now they were still in the dark. She asked him how he knew the family. He picked his words carefully, not wanting to associate his father with Leila. The two people murdered were Leila's mother and her daughter, he believed. He broke down as it was all too much for him to take in, and just seeing Leila lying there in a shocked state didn't help. He had just lost his half-sister, but he didn't disclose this. He reached for her hand. He felt she needed to be touched to let her know someone was there for her. The questions kept coming: where did Leila live, what did she do, how old was the little girl and where was the father? The last question he dismissed; it was not up for discussion. The policewoman could see he was hurting so finished the questioning for the time being. Tomorrow was another day!

Mitchell sat holding Leila's hand. He worried that she would wake up remembering what she had last seen, which is why he felt he had to be there for her. The nurse told him to go the cafeteria and get something to eat, as it would be closing soon, but he feared she might wake while he was gone.

It wasn't long after that he felt her hand grasping his, so he signalled to the nurse. They both waited, hoping to see some movement in her eyes, but no, that didn't happen. Mitchell moved his other hand and lay it on top of Leila's, hoping to get her to respond, but her eyes stayed closed. He drifted off taking little naps, as he had had a long day. During one of his naps, he woke to hear sobbing. There was Leila sitting up in bed staring into the unknown, silently weeping. Mitchell jumped up and sat on her bed and put his arms around her. She buried her head into him and let the tears flow. He didn't know how much she remembered so stayed silent. The nurse sat and watched as she didn't want to interrupt; it was better for Leila to express the sadness that had encumbered her.

"Where am I?" were her first words. Mitchell told her she was in hospital as she was in shock.

"I had a terrible dream that I had lost Willow, but that's not true, is it?" What could Mitchell say? The truth had to be told; it couldn't be hidden.

"Yes, Leila, Willow has been taken, so has your mother. Burglars broke into the home and took their lives. Let your grief out. Don't bottle it up."

On hearing this, a loud scream echoed through the hospital. It wasn't a dream, it was true. Why did she think it was a dream? Was it because that's what she wanted it to be?

Mitchell held on to her as she sobbed uncontrollably.

No one spoke. It was time to let all her emotions out as she was suffering deep down. How else was she to deal with such a horrific truth?

The nurse left the room and it was then Mitchell introduced himself.

"I knew it was you by your voice," she sobbed. After her initial waking Leila dropped back into a deep sleep. Mitchell did wonder if she had taken everything in, but only time would tell. The doctor who was assigned to Leila was pleased to hear she had come to, although what she had to face was daunting. He was told a friend was with her, so he would look in on her on his rounds. There were reporters hanging around outside the hospital trying to get a story from the police, but all the news they were given was it was a bungled burglary, and two bodies were found. No names had been released. The police wanted to talk to the survivor to see what she wanted the press to know. The bodies had been taken to the mortuary, pending instructions as to what to do.

This morning Leila woke and sat up in bed. She had worked out what was to happen. She didn't want any names released; it was to be kept within the remaining family. When the police superintendent came to talk to her, she asked that name suppression remain as she was the only living relative. She didn't want to experience the media following her wherever she went. She had had to deal with that once before; never again.

Mitchell had left her bedside last night as he needed some sleep. He went out to the property where the solicitor had dropped his bags and found a spare room, so dossed down for the night. He hoped Leila wouldn't mind. He hadn't thought much about what was going to happen to the property, now that Willow was deceased, as they were the two beneficiaries.

Back at the murder scene the police were still trying to work out why the burglars chose this particular home. Were they tipped off by someone? One of the officers on duty was studying the photos on the wall as he thought he recognised one of the faces. Why did he think he knew her, he racked his brain, but still couldn't fathom a connection. It was only a couple of minutes later when it all fell into place, as he was one of the officers asked to protect a young lady who was being harassed by reporters as she was a victim of rape. Yes, that's where he had seen her before. Was the little girl who was murdered the outcome of the rape? Was there a connection here? He felt sick. How was she ever going to recover from this horrific ordeal? He felt he had to mention this to his superior. He thanked the officer and said they were to keep this under wraps; he didn't want it circulating among other staff.

The next morning when the doctor came to Leila's bedside, he sat down and asked her how she thought she would manage, as she had a huge hurdle to overcome. "I will give you a prescription for some pills which I want you to take, just to get you over the initial shock."

Leila was overcome by his kind manner. "I am trying to think things through, but I don't know where to start. I have lost my whole family, my mother and my daughter," she sobbed.

The doctor took her hand and squeezed it. "I believe

you have a friend. Lean on him and he will help you get through this. But please take the medication I have prescribed, as you can't manage this without a little help. Good luck, my dear."

Tears streamed down Leila's cheeks as she thought what was ahead, with funerals to organise, then life on her own. Mitchell had told her not to worry, as if she told him what she wanted, he would arrange it all. The hospital wanted her to stay another night as the police wanted to talk with her. Up to now the hospital staff had protected her and wouldn't let her be interviewed until they thought she could handle questions. She had to be allowed time to grieve.

The police chief introduced himself and asked if she was ready to answer questions. Leila nodded in reply. "This will be painful for you, but we need to know why these murders occurred. Do you know if anyone would want revenge on your mother?" Leila let him know she was a quiet person who kept very much to herself, so she couldn't think there would be a motive. He replied, "At this stage we have no idea who went into the home or how many people were involved; that is the frustrating thing. Did your mother have any valuables?" Leila explained she had a lot of nice jewellery but apart from that she couldn't think of anything else, apart from the car. It was often admired by people. "Yes, the car would be a drawcard to younger persons. We are in the dark at this stage, so we have put out a watch to all police stations. We have changed the locks on the doors, so no one has been able to enter the home apart from the police. We have steam cleaned the floors, so there is no evidence of anything that happened. My men are searching the neighbourhoods to see if anyone noticed strange happenings within the last few days. We have put out an alert on the car so are hoping someone comes forward. At this stage we have nothing to go on, but should that change, we will be in contact with you. Please don't go there on your own; take someone with you. Here are the new keys," he said to Leila.

She told him she was not ready to go there yet, but she had her own place to go to.

Then the penny dropped: it was not her home any more as it was left to Willow and Mitchell. Now that Willow had gone, she had no claim on it. This brought on more tears. The police officer asked if he could be of any help, but this was private, something she wasn't ready to discuss, so politely let him know. "I will leave now, and as soon as we have any news, we will be in touch. Goodbye, Leila."

Mitchell was Leila's next visitor. She told him of the police visit and that there were no clues as to why the burglars had been drawn to her mother's home, other than perhaps the car. "If the car was the main reason, it almost points to younger persons, but why take lives? They must have panicked," he replied. Leila had now been in hospital four days and cried an ocean of tears.

"I have been to the funeral home; it is time for you to arrange whatever you want for your loved ones. I want you to see them. Willow looks beautiful. I am so sad this was my first meeting with her," said a tearful Mitchell.

Just hearing these words once again brought a flood of tears from Leila. "I don't know what to do. All I can think of is I just want the two of us to say goodbye, as I want this to be a private affair."

"I will come and pick you up in the morning, then we will go to the funeral parlour together. I hope you don't mind; I have been staying at your place, but tomorrow I will find somewhere else to live," Mitchell told her.

This brought a protest from Leila. "No, Mitchell, this is your place and now that Willow has gone, I will move out."

Mitchell was shocked to hear that she thought this way. "Leila, my father did you a grave injustice and I insist Willow's share becomes your share. You were the one who bore the brunt of humiliation for his wrongdoing. No way will you be moving out; it is your home. I will find somewhere else." Leila told him they would discuss this further tomorrow.

That night as she lay in the hospital bed she thought of Mitchell. She would be lonely out there on her own, so perhaps they could both live there as it was a large home. She would feel safer with him on the property, especially at the moment. Leila had her mother's home, but to live there after what happened would be a sorry reminder of that fateful day. One day she would have to face that prospect, but that was certainly not now. Her mind was closed on any thought of entering that home.

Mitchell carried Leila's bag to the car. There was very little in it because of her rushed trip to hospital. Reporters were hovering around trying to get a story, not knowing that it was her they were after. He settled her in the car then climbed in himself. Before he started the engine he leaned over and took her hand. "We are going to the funeral parlour; you must say goodbye. I know it will be sad but please be brave. While we are there, we will make funeral arrangements for them to be buried."

Leila tried to hold on to her grief, but it was all too much. Mitchell let her cry her heart out and he did wonder how she would react upon seeing the bodies. As they pulled up at the funeral home, he walked around and opened the car door. He put his arms around her and walked her into the building where the undertaker was waiting for them, as Mitchell had let him know in advance. He led them to where the bodies lay in their coffins. An inner strength took over and she asked for a chair to be placed between the coffins so she could sit and say her final farewells. She asked to be left on her own, so the two men left the room. Mitchell spoke with the funeral director making the final arrangements. He arranged for a celebrant to be there tomorrow, when a private ceremony would be held.

As they left the funeral parlour Mitchell asked Leila if she wanted to go to her mother's home, but she told him she wasn't ready, so they drove out to their acreage. Mitchell had gathered up all Willow's toys along with the ones he had brought back for her and put them in the toybox which he had moved into a corner in the lounge. It was heartbreaking that she was not there, but photos adorned the walls making it feel she was still present. As Leila walked around the home her heart felt empty. She knew she had to put the past behind her, but that was easier said than done. It was her future she had to concentrate on, as she had missed a week of class so it would have to be caught up on.

Mitchell brought her a cup of coffee and asked her to sit down so they could talk. "I want you to stay here, Leila. This is your home; I will find somewhere else."

"But Mitchell, this is your home too. Could you please stay here with me as I feel afraid on my own? My mind has not settled yet. I need you here," pleaded Leila. This plea was taken on board, as he knew himself she was not ready to cope on her own, and she needed company.

The funeral was over and Leila felt empty. How was she going to move forward and put the past behind her? Saying goodbye to her little girl took all the energy she had left, and she just wanted to curl up and die. If not for Mitchell supporting her, she would not have been able to cope on her own.

The solicitor and two police personnel had come to the service as they wanted to speak with Leila afterwards. They told her they had questioned the neighbours, and several had come up with valuable information. One neighbour in particular had seen what looked like a middle-aged man at the back of the house peering in the windows and he took off when he noticed her looking at him. Also, the neighbour on the other side had been visited by a man who had asked questions about the occupant of the house. The police had taken both of these witnesses into the station, so they could get a forensic artist to draw a rough image of the stranger that was hanging around. Then they would circulate it in the *Gold Coast Bulletin* with hopes someone might come forward.

Mitchell had a vested interest in this case outside of Leila, as he had passed his final exams and was now a qualified forensic scientist, which meant he could collaborate with law enforcement to investigate certain crimes and analyse evidence to determine what had happened. He kept this information to himself as he was personally involved in the case.

Leila was now back at university as she had a lot of catching up to do. She was grateful Mitchell had agreed to stay in the house with her, as she dreaded to think what would have happened if she was on her own. She still had not been back to her mother's home as it was all still too raw for her to go there. Today being Saturday, the police rang and asked if they could come out to her home, to which she told them she would be there all day. When they arrived, they brought with them an image of a man who they thought might be a likely suspect. Leila looked at the image; she felt she had seen that face before, but where? Before she could answer, the policewoman interrupted, "We had a call from the manager of the Marina Mirage resort. Some of his staff recognised a likeness to a guest who had been staying with them. He was from New Zealand." As soon as New Zealand was mentioned, Leila immediately realised this was the man she spoke with at Sea World, the man who asked to take her photo. But why?

Back in Dunedin

Reece arrived at Lily's as he was worried that perhaps the two murdered victims were connected to Lee Lee. How would he find out, as no names were mentioned in connection with the murders? He brought with him a pile of newspapers that he had sifted through, but still no information was forthcoming. The only little piece that he related to was that tragedy had struck this family twice in a short while. This raised Reece's suspicions as he knew Lee Lee had been raped. That was the first, and the murders, were they the second? Lily had to tell Reece to calm down, as he had no evidence that this all pertained to Lee Lee. "Don't take it into your own hands, Reece. There is nothing we can do from here. I'm sure if she was involved in this terrible murder we would have known by now."

"But how would we know? No one associates us with her," replied an upset Reece.

Lily thought on this for a moment. He was right; no one knew the connection if this was in fact Leila.

"I am going back to Australia," Reece said, with some anger in his voice. "I've made up my mind. This is unsettling me and I have to find out for myself. Now I know where Amelia lives, I will arrive unannounced then she can't fob me off."

Lily could not believe how convinced he was that there was a connection somewhere in this case. "If you wait for two weeks, the case I am presiding over will be finished and I will come with you," she told him. This was music to his ears; was this the start to winning her back? He missed her so much. Perhaps she was missing him, he told himself. But this was a long way from the truth, especially in Lily's mind.

The case before the courts that Lily was presiding over was a civil court case, but she was asked to handle it because they were so far behind in that department. It entailed gold-mining rights, something she knew nothing about, so a lot of research had to be done. An old-timer had the rights to three claims which he thought he held for life, but on his arrival one day he was confronted by several men who had set up sluice boxes and were working his claim. When he asked who had given them authority to mine his patch, he was told the Land Board had granted them prospecting rights and they had licences to prove this. On hearing this, the old-timer thought he had been double-crossed so he was taking on the government Lands & Survey Department. Lily had done her homework on the laws governing the land, something she had never come across before, and consequently her family hadn't seen much of her over the past week.

The hearing was in its final week, so a verdict had to be reached. What the old-timer hadn't read into his mining rights was the fact that if he had left the claim unattended for a period longer than twelve months, it became tenable again to other interested parties seeking claims. Although he had another two claims, this was his most profitable one. He had taken time out because of ill health, but this did not stand up in court. Regardless of ill health, the law was the law.

Lily listened to both sides of the case and although she felt sorry for the old-timer she could not change the law, so a decision was made, and the claim went to the new prospectors. She loved the variety of cases that came before the courts, as it gave her an insight as to how the law held the final decision.

Lily wanted to hold a family meeting to discuss her pending trip with Reece to Australia. Mackenzie was still studying journalism at university, while Harrison was making his mark, as all talk at the moment was on microskills and microcredentials in areas spanning artificial intelligence, cyber security, cloud computing and data analytics. These courses were needed in order to meet increasing demands and skills for a strong and safe digital economy. Microcredentials make things happen quickly. They are short courses enabling people to upskill or retrain in short periods of time, getting them into the workforce faster. Harrison was right into this as it did away with years of study. Microcredentials were standalone formal awards that recognise your skills and knowledge in a particular area, which is becoming increasingly important in the digital world. Nano-learning involves delivering information in a condensed and digestible format, often digitally, within a period shorter than 10 minutes. This was all music to Harrison's ears, as it gave him specific skill recognition in a much quicker time. All his spare time was spent gaming. He had friends from all around the world through his gaming knowledge, and at night whatever time when he sat down at his computer, someone was waiting for him to join in online gaming.

Eventually Lily managed to drag the children away from their distractions and got them to sit at the table for a family talk. She informed them of her plan to go to Australia with Reece as he was convinced the murders that had happened were somehow connected to the girl he met at the theme park.

Kennedy thought this was a good idea as Lily needed a break away from her work. He was not the slightest bit worried that Reece and Lily would be together, as he knew Lily's love was reserved for him, and him only.

Reece would have to talk hard to his boss to ask for another week's holiday, but by the time the air tickets were booked it wouldn't happen for at least another two weeks. For Lily it was the right time, as there was a break before court resumed.

It was now time to say their goodbyes as Reece and Lily were about to proceed through customs. Kennedy,

Harrison and Mackenzie were there to see them off and wish them luck with tracking down Amelia and finding out if Reece's premonitions rang true. Kennedy took Lily in his arms and placed her hand on his heart. She knew what this meant, as it was his way of saying she belonged to him totally and their love was forever.

"Would all passengers on flight NZ 247 to Brisbane please proceed to boarding at Gate 10." This announcement was the final call, so Lily yelled, "Goodbye family," and joined the queue.

As the plane approached Brisbane, Reece was woken by the announcement they would be landing in 10 minutes. He turned to Lily and asked, "Have I been asleep for long?"

"Yes, your eyes have been closed for two hours."

Reece had been dreaming of spending the next week with Lily. He had booked two connecting rooms with high hopes he might be invited to her bed. They were staying at the Marina Mirage resort, Reece's favourite accommodation on the Gold Coast. It was within walking distance of Amelia's home.

"You know, Lily, Amelia is going to get a shock when we turn up at her door. I think the relationship ended years ago and she didn't want us to know. Do you think he might have absconded with some of her money and she feels bad about it?"

Lily didn't know what to think. She couldn't get her head around the fact that Amelia had lied to Reece. Suddenly the plane hit the tarmac and the screech of brakes let them know they had landed. Once through customs they were to get on the train to Robina station where a shuttle would be waiting for them to take them to their destination.

As they left the aircraft and walked the long corridor to line up at customs, they noticed a heavy police attendance throughout the airport. "There is something strange going on here?" remarked Lily. Reece agreed with her, as he had never seen so many police at any airport he had been to. "Perhaps there was a criminal on our flight and they are waiting for him," he remarked. Lily shuddered; thank goodness they had arrived safely.

Leila had been in contact with real estate agents regarding the sale of Amelia's home, but no one was interested once they were given the address. There was a stigma due to the murders that had happened there. It was suggested it be bulldozed down so a new home and a new life could begin from scratch. The section itself was worth a lot of money. This news made Leila cry as she thought back over the wonderful years she had lived there with her mother. She remembered she helped choose the property, although she couldn't remember where they lived before they bought that home. As yet she hadn't been back, so Mitchell suggested it was time for her to return there and make some decisions on what was to happen to the contents. He was surprised that no solicitor had been in touch with her, as surely her mother had left a will.

"Leila, do you know who your mother's solicitors are?" he asked.

She looked blankly at him. "No, Mitchell, I have no idea. We never discussed financial matters. Perhaps there might be something among her personal papers that will tell us," she suggested.

"Okay, then let's go there now while we are on the subject. Get ready and I will take you."

Leila braced herself, as she had been avoiding this visit but agreed that it had to happen.

As they entered the home a stillness prevailed. Leila stood in the dining room, which was the last place she had seen the bodies. She turned to Mitchell and held on to him, burying her head in his chest and trying to hide her tears. "That's where it happened," she sobbed. "They were lying there on the floor in a pool of blood."

Mitchell cradled her in his arms. He could see she was heartbroken; would she ever mend? "Come, Leila, please try and be strong. Let's take down the photos of Willow and your mother. We can put them on the walls in our home where their memories will live on."

She told Mitchell the ones to take so he put them in a box. What would she do without him? He was now a big part of her life, in fact her only rock.

Mitchell noticed a lot of valuable ornaments so asked if she wanted to take some of them. She picked up several, the ones that held memories, but the rest she would leave. "I will leave everything else in this room, including the furniture, to the Salvation Army. They can come and pick it up."

The next move was to her mother's bedroom where there was a walk-in wardrobe full of beautiful clothes and shoes. This was the breaking point, as here were all her mother's belongings never to be worn by her again. Leila fell to her knees and sobbed as she looked at the clothes, the memories of her mother wearing them flashing before her eyes. "What will I do with them, Mitchell?" she cried. "When I look at them all I can see is Mother. Please help me."

Mitchell was so moved by this sorrowful creature before him, he sat down and took her in his arms and held her sobbing body. At this moment he knew he could never leave her; she needed him and he wanted her. They held each other until she felt she could carry on.

The jewellery was next. There were so many expensive-looking pieces, Mitchell said he would put it all in a box and take it with them and when she felt the time was right to sift through it, it was there for her. He asked her about the clothes, even suggested they be put in the car and be sorted through at a later date when she could make the right decision.

Leila walked over to a desk where Amelia kept her personal papers, which were in files, so she asked Mitchell to put the files in the car, and she would attend to them later.

The hardest moment was about to be faced and that was Willow's bedroom. Hanging from the ceiling were mobiles of stars and fairies, and along the floor were toys of all shapes and sizes. It was plain to see Amelia spoilt her granddaughter and that was evident here in this room today. She had her own wardrobe of beautiful clothes. It was all too much; Leila ran from the room. Mitchell knew he had to take over, so he put the clothes and the mobiles in a box. The toys he would leave with the cot and the furniture to go to the Salvation Army, as they could sell a lot of the gear and make good money.

After the boxes were loaded into the car, he went back several times to gather some of Amelia's clothes and lay them on top of everything. He then asked Leila to see if she wanted to take anything else, but all she wanted to do was leave the property. She asked Mitchell if he would ring the Salvation Army and tell them to take what they wanted, before the building was demolished. It was going to take Leila a long time to get her head around the home being destroyed, but as she thought about it, the legacy it left was not a pretty one!

Now that everything Leila decided to keep was at the acreage, Mitchell had put it all into one room, so she could go through it when she felt ready. But he was insistent that she read through her mother's personal files. He brought them out and sat them on the occasional table and asked her to start on them. The first item she picked up was an envelope with just 'Amelia' written on it. This obviously hadn't come by post as it had no address. She opened it and pondered over what she was reading.

'Amelia, please get in touch with us. We need your phone number. I called several times but there was no answer, and I'm leaving to go back to New Zealand today. Reece.'

What did all this mean? Who was Reece and how did he know her mother? She knew no one in New Zealand.

Leila put this aside as it made no sense. As she sorted through more papers, she found a letter from a solicitor's asking Amelia to come into their office as they wanted her to update some papers. She gave it to Mitchell and asked him to contact them. "But, Leila, it might be personal information that perhaps I shouldn't know about," he said.

"Mitchell you are all I have left; I feel you are part of me. I have nothing to hide, so please help me?"

For a moment he couldn't believe what he had just heard. 'You are part of me.' What did she mean by this? He knew by now his feelings went way beyond being just friends; he had fallen for her, and she tore at his heart. Many times, when he held her in his arms, he wanted to kiss her and let her know how he felt, but it was all too soon for her to hear this.

"If you want me to get in touch with the solicitor's office I will go tomorrow while you are at varsity."

Leila thanked him and continued sorting through the files. When she saw the bank statements, she couldn't believe her mother had so much money invested. There were millions of dollars, but how did she have so much money, as Leila could never remember her ever working and she certainly spent plenty. It was then that she realised her mother had never spoken about her past, and she knew nothing beyond their lives together. Her mother always lived in the present, and nothing nostalgic was ever talked about. Leila didn't know if Amelia was an only child, or anything about her family, as she never mentioned anyone else. She just presumed there were only the two of them. They had lived a busy life together and it was only now she realised there hadn't been time for a man in her mother's life, and she never seemed much interested in the opposite sex. It was only now she realised Amelia's life was built around herself and Willow, but why? She mentioned this to Mitchell who was as surprised as herself.

"Don't you know anything about your background?" he asked.

Leila thought on this and, no, she knew nothing beyond her life with her mother.

Today while Leila was at varsity, Mitchell made his way to the solicitor's address that Leila had given him. He was shown into an office of a Mr Jarrad, who apparently was Amelia's solicitor. After their greetings Mitchell asked him why he hadn't been in touch with Amelia's daughter after her death.

"What do you mean, after her death?" asked the solicitor. He had no idea Amelia had passed away and was shocked. Mitchell told him Amelia and her granddaughter were murdered over a month ago. It hit Mr Jarrad like a tornado. He had read about the murders but as no names were released, he knew nothing more, certainly not associating it with any of his clients. He hadn't seen a death notice in the paper, as he read this page every day. He remembered he had two letters written by Amelia, one for her daughter on her death and the other was to be sent to an address in New Zealand.

"Why have you come instead of Amelia's daughter?" the solicitor asked. Mitchell told him Leila was in a distressed state after her horrific losses and he was only acting on her instructions.

"I'm sorry, I can't pass the letter on to you as I was asked to give it to her personally; these were Amelia's instructions," he told Mitchell politely. Mitchell said he would bring Leila in as soon as she thought she was ready.

"I have Amelia's will here so I will read it to her when she comes in. She was a very wealthy lady thanks to her father who apparently left all his money to her. She had it transferred to an Australian bank when she and her daughter shifted over here from New Zealand. I think the daughter was about five or six years old when they brought the canal block home. I remember Amelia saying her daughter helped her choose it.

"They seemed a lovely family. But there was never any mention of a father. Thank you for putting me in the picture. I feel sick not knowing that all the time I knew the murdered family. Just get Leila to ring me when she is ready to speak with me."

Mitchell thanked him and left the office. He sat in his car and tried to understand what he had been told about Leila's background. Obviously she had no idea. When the solicitor mentioned New Zealand, he remembered Leila wondering about the letter of her mother's, written by someone from there, as she just dismissed it, thinking they had no ties with anyone from New Zealand. Was her mother hiding a secret? Tonight, when they were talking, he would drop some hints to Leila and see what she knew.

Mitchell stopped off and picked up some take-aways for tea. He had called Leila and told her not to worry about cooking anything; he would bring something home. While they were sitting at the table, Mitchell asked her if she had ever been to New Zealand. No, she didn't think so, as they had lived in Australia all their lives.

"Did your mother ever live there?"

Leila said she didn't think so, as she had never spoken about living there, and she just presumed she was Australian. This confirmed to Mitchell that Amelia had not told her daughter the truth. What secrets was she hiding from her?

"Why are you asking me all these questions? You haven't told me what the solicitor had to say?" she quizzed.

Mitchell told her there was a letter at the office for her from her mother on her death, and it was to be given to her personally, on her mother's request. There was also one to go to someone in New Zealand. "That's why I asked you about New Zealand." Leila thought nothing more about this.

When the reservation came through to the Marina Mirage for a Mr Reece McMahon from New Zealand, the receptionist rang the manager, as the staff had seen the image that was circulating after the murders. The manager rang the police straight away to let them know the suspect was returning to the Gold Coast on a certain day. This got the police hot on the trail, contacting the airport to confirm that this traveller was booked on a certain flight. They arranged to be at the airport on his arrival. A plan was put in place by the police. Because they wanted to keep this under wraps, not wanting it out in the public, two undercover police officers would travel on the same transport as the suspect until they reached their destination.

Arriving in Australia

As Reece and Lily made their way through customs, they were aware of a large police contingent throughout the airport. People were commenting to each other and even asking others if they knew what was happening. Lily felt a little on edge; what was this all about? They went to the carousel to gather their luggage and still they couldn't shake them off. Reece asked Lily to stay put while he made enquiries about the train timetable. It was then she thought Reece was in their sights, as when he came back, they seemed to be right behind him. Was she just imagining this, what would the police want with Reece?

She decided not to say anything as he might get upset and cause a scene. Once through customs, they walked to the station just outside the airport and along with many other people they got on the train to Surfers Paradise. No uniformed police were in sight, so Lily breathed a sigh of relief.

At the Robina station, a courtesy coach was waiting to pick up passengers who were staying at Marina Mirage. Several groups of visitors climbed aboard with their luggage, but there were two men who appeared not to have luggage but boarded the coach. They sat behind Reece and Lily. Halfway into the trip Reece spoke with one of the men and asked him how long they were staying at the Marina Mirage. This brought a little hesitation, then a stutter, "I'm…. not sure, depends on our business." This signalled to Reece the conversation was finished so he turned to the couple opposite. "Where are you from?" he asked. When they said they were from Wanaka, this was the start of an ongoing conversation.

The highway from Robina to Seaworld Drive was very busy so the journey was at a slow pace. Reece told Lily their first job tomorrow was to walk to 17 Fernside Drive and surprise Amelia. "I can't wait to see the look on her face when we front up. This time she won't be able to fob me off; she will have to answer some questions," he assured Lily.

As the coach pulled up outside reception, two cars stopped right beside it and out climbed six police officers. The coach driver told his passengers to remain seated. Suddenly the two men behind Reece and Lily came forward and told Reece to stand up. Within minutes he was in handcuffs and being led off the coach. Lily watched in shock. Everything happened so quick; what had Reece done? Next thing the cars drove off with Reece inside.

"You are free to go now," the driver told his remaining passengers. All eyes were on Lily.

She climbed off the bus and waited for the driver to offload her and Reece's suitcases. "Do you know what has happened, why has Reece been taken away?" she asked. The driver looked at her; how was he meant to know? "All I know is the police alerted me that they were to pick up a suspect off my bus. Sorry, lady."

A suspect, what did he mean? "What is he a suspect for?"

"I told you lady. I know nothing?"

The bellboy was there with his trolley loading her cases. "Follow me, Madam." In a shocked state Lily did as she was asked.

Once in her suite, as soon as her hands were free, she rummaged through her bag to find her phone. She had to talk to Kennedy. "Kennedy, something terrible has happened. Reece has been arrested and taken away in handcuffs by the police. I don't know what for. What will I do?" she sobbed. "I don't know where they have taken him, or how to contact him."

"Lily, calm down, there must be some mistake. What would the police want with Reece? It must be mistaken identity. Try and relax, have something to eat. If it is not sorted by morning, ring me, my darling."

Lily couldn't control her emotions. "I just wish you were here with me, so I could put my hand on your heart and feel the warmth between us. I'm a judge and yet I feel so powerless, new country and new surroundings, I feel so lost." Kennedy told her not to panic and to be strong.

By the morning he was sure it would all be over. "What did you have planned for tomorrow?" he asked. Lily explained they were going to walk to Amelia's home and surprise her. With this, Kennedy told her to have an early night as she would feel better after a good sleep.

When Lily woke, she was surprised she had slept all night. She must have been exhausted by all that had happened yesterday. What was her first move today? She decided to call Reece on his cell phone, but this met with no joy. Next was the local police station. She walked down to reception and asked the guy behind the desk for the phone number of the local police. He looked at Lily and asked if something was wrong. She didn't want to feel embarrassed so said everything was fine, if she could just have the number. On receiving this, she went back to her suite and phoned. Well, that was a total waste of time. They couldn't tell her anything as an arrest by police was out of their hands, especially when she couldn't tell them what it was about. "Where do I go from here?" she asked. They said they would follow it up and would call her when they had some information. She made sure they had her phone number, having repeated it several times. Now what would she do? Perhaps she could walk to Amelia's, and they could sort something out there. She might be able to help Lily; she needed a friend.

Lily asked at reception how she would find Fernside Drive, so she was given a map. The receptionist drew a red line on the streets she was to follow. Lily thanked her and left the resort to begin her walk. She felt perhaps she could talk to Amelia on her own and find out why she lied to Reece. As she followed the red line her eyes were on her phone, but there was no news from Reece or the police. After ten minutes she found herself in Fernside Drive, where she knew she was looking for number 17. As she made her way towards number 17 all that was there was an empty section. She stopped and scratched her head. Where had the house gone? She tracked back to see if she had the right number. Yes, the one before was 15 and the one after was 19.

While standing there in a stunned state she was disturbed by a voice, "Can I help you? That section is for sale, are you interested in it?" Lily said no, before she had time to think. "I don't blame you; this is where the murders happened, so they bulldozed the house down. I'm not meant to tell people this, but I would like to know the history before I bought it, especially seeing it was so gruesome."

"What murders?" asked Lily.

"Oh, a grandmother and her granddaughter were murdered there. They were found by the little girl's mother when she came to pick her up after finishing varsity."

On hearing this Lily let out a squeal. This was too much for her to handle, and she walked along to the neighbours and sat on the fence. She couldn't believe what she had been told.

"Are you okay?" asked the stranger.

"I'm in shock. I think I knew the lady who lived there. Did you know her name?" asked Lily. The stranger didn't know but said the lady in number 19 had lived in this street for many years and perhaps she might know. Apparently, she kept to herself, and didn't mix with many people. Lily thanked the stranger and said she might visit number 19 when she had gathered her thoughts. With this the stranger headed off.

Lily sat in silence; she was still trying to get her head around what happened. Then she panicked. If Amelia lived here then she was a murder victim, but who was the child? The stranger said it was her granddaughter, but she didn't have any children, or did she? They really knew nothing of her life in Australia, only that she had met a man on the internet and was living with him, so perhaps there was a granddaughter. No, that couldn't be right as she wasn't old enough to have one, or her daughter must have been very young when she had a baby, in fact a young teenager. Then something came to her mind. Reece did say about a young surf lifesaver who was raped when just a teenager. It all seemed bizarre. Were there connections? She had to find out.

Lily waited until her head had come back down to earth, then she made her way to house number 19. She stood and ran her hands through her hair hoping she looked okay, then she knocked on the door. A few moments later a lady appeared. Lily introduced herself and asked if she could talk to her. "I'm sorry if I am interrupting, but I need some information on the lady who lived in the home next door. I have just been told there was a murder there, and the reason I'm enquiring is I think she is related to me. Could you please tell me her name?"

The neighbour said she was Amelia Hammond. This is not the answer Lily wanted to hear. "And the little girl, who was she?"

"She was her granddaughter," replied the neighbour.

"I didn't realise that Amelia and her partner had children," remarked Lily.

The neighbour looked surprised. "No, Amelia never had a partner. She and her little girl came over from New Zealand and bought this home. She kept to herself and doted on her daughter; they were inseparable."

Lily couldn't take this in.

"But Amelia never had a daughter in New Zealand. Do you know her daughter's name?" Lily asked.

"Yes, her name is Leila."

Lily covered her face with her hands as a loud sob escaped. The neighbour came over and comforted her. "Are you alright?"

Through her sobs Lily asked how old the little girl was, when they came to live next door. When she was told Leila was about six, her sobs turned to hysteria. The neighbour didn't know what to say or do, so she sat with her arms around her. In all this Lily managed to work out that Amelia's granddaughter was not hers, but was Lily's, and now she was gone. But where was Leila?

When Lily gained her composure, she apologised. "I'm so sorry for my outburst. I can't believe what I've just heard. We had our little girl stolen from us in New Zealand nearly eighteen years ago and her name was Leila. Amelia was my husband's half-sister and she lived in Dunedin where we lived. Not once did we connect Leila's disappearance with Amelia, but now that I know, it was so easy for her to steal her. It has been classed as a cold case for all these years. We were led to believe that Amelia had met a man on the internet and came over here to live with him. They travelled around in a campervan picking up work here and there, so we were unable to contact her unless she called us. Do you know where Leila lives? She must be a mess having lost her so-called mother and her daughter."

The neighbour told Lily she didn't know where Leila moved to, but she could not stay next door with all the reporters and the press hounding her for days when her name got out as the victim of rape, by a trusted member of the lifesaving community.

This was all too much. What had their Leila gone through when she wasn't there to comfort her? Tears flowed uncontrollably. This was worse than a nightmare; it was a true-life horror. Lily remembered her as the little girl who gave them so much love and hope.

The neighbour made Lily a cup of tea to help comfort her after learning of so much sadness. It was now that Lily wanted to know first-hand what had actually happened next door. She was told how it was a burglary gone wrong. The little girl had died in her grandmother's arms as they both had suffered bullet wounds. Suddenly Lily gained an inner strength and was able to absorb what she was being told, although it was horrific. At the end she asked if the robbers had been caught.

"No, there were no leads until a neighbour came forward, as she had seen a middle-aged man peeping in the windows several days before the murders. I think he was the same man who came here enquiring about the health of the man next door, as he had called several times and no one answered the door. I told him no man lived there. He thought they were house-sitting for friends."

As soon as house-sitting was mentioned Lily knew this was Reece.

"Is he a suspect?" Lily asked.

"Yes, an image has been circulating, apparently he is from New Zealand, and the police are on to him."

Suddenly everything started falling into place. Was that why they were being watched the moment they arrived at the airport? In this moment Lily saw the funny side; it was almost laughable, Reece of all people a suspect in a murder! Her anxiety over him disappeared. It would all be sorted soon.

Lily's mind went back to her main concern, that of her stolen daughter. At this moment in time, she hated Amelia for stealing Leila. Fancy doing that to her own flesh and blood! She knew the pain they were all going through, but now that reality struck, she was no longer here. Lily just wanted to be on her own, to digest all that had happened in her own silent space. She stood up and hugged her host and thanked her. "If you want to come back and talk some more, I'll be here," she told Lily.

As soon as Lily was on her own, she couldn't stop the stream of tears as they flooded down her cheeks. She didn't know if they were tears of joy or tears of sorrow. She had found Leila, but in the process lost a granddaughter. Her legs felt like jelly; she had to sit down and there in front of her was a bus shelter. Her mind was all over the place, she couldn't focus, shock had set in, all she could do was cry her heart out.

Lily didn't know how long she was there, but the sun had gone down. Then she felt her phone vibrating in her purse, by the time she got it out, it had stopped. There were messages from Kennedy asking her to call him. First, she had to try to contact Reece as he was Leila's father, to let him know their daughter was stolen by Amelia and was living here in Surfers Paradise. An inner strength told Lily she could face this head on, she was a survivor. Look at all the cases she had presided over. Many were full of heartaches never to be solved, but this one was going to be solved!

On her arrival back at the resort, a police officer was waiting for her. He could see she was upset by her red swollen eyes. "Are you alright?" he asked her. This started Lily off again; of course she was not alright.

"Where is Reece? You took him away without an explanation. I'm a High Court judge in New Zealand, and this was not acceptable behaviour."

The police officer was very apologetic. "We are releasing him later, as we have had a breakthrough. A crashed Ferrari was found in the hinterland among some gum trees with a body still inside. I just need a statement from you, to verify who Reece is."

Lily told him her predicament and how she had just found out the murdered victims were family members.

"Oh, I'm sorry but it was the wishes of the remaining family member not to have any names released," he stated.

"I will have you know the remaining family member is my daughter who was stolen from us over sixteen years ago. She was stolen from Auckland Airport. Can you please tell me where we can find her? I need to hold her," sobbed Lily.

But the officer could not give out any information without Leila's permission. "I know this is hard for you, but I am under instructions from higher authorities, and as a judge you will know the procedure." Lily nodded her head. At least Leila was still alive; the rest would follow.

Now it was time to call Kennedy, as there were another two calls from him. She made her way up to her suite, opened the door, walked to her bedroom and fell onto the bed exhausted. She needed a moment to reflect on all the day's happenings, but her phone put an end to that. "Hi Kennedy, I have had a day from hell. I have missed you, my darling. You are not going to believe what you are about to hear." Lily explained her day as best she could, from start to finish.

Kennedy was shocked to hear it was Amelia who had stollen Leila, as he had placed so much faith in her. "So what she told Reece were lies. By the way, where is he?"

Lily told him Reece was being released tonight. "I don't think he knows about Leila and that his premonitions about the murders were true. I guess I will find out soon. Can you imagine how happy he will be, to know he has his daughter back? Please tell Mackenzie and Harrison their sister is alive. What breaks my heart is she has been on her own through this horrific time; my heart bleeds for her Kennedy," she sobbed.

He told her to take one day at a time, that the hardest part was over, and it could only get better. "I wish I could be with you, but it is best you and Reece, as her father, meet her, otherwise she might be confused. I miss you my darling, but my hand is on your heart, it will never leave."

"Oh, Kennedy, that's what I love about you, you say words with so much meaning, you are my forever love. Goodnight my darling."

Just as Lily was about to get something to eat there was a knock on her door and when she opened it there stood Reece. They embraced each other. It was so good to be back together, and now they could carry on. Who was going to talk first? Of course it was Reece. "Thank God they found the crashed car with a body inside, or I might have still been in the lock-up."

Lily had news for him, so asked him to sit down. By the time she had finished relaying the day's findings, Reece was shedding tears. What he had imagined for all those weeks had been linked to the girl and her daughter who he had met at Sea World. She was Leila and he had actually met his little granddaughter who was no longer alive. "Lily, I actually spoke with our granddaughter. She pinched a chip out of my pottle and to think she is no longer with us, how sad. I still have the photo of the two of them watching the dolphin display. When do you think we can meet Leila?" he asked.

This was a hard question; it would have to be thought through with Leila's best interest at heart. As much as Lily wanted to cuddle her and tell her she loved her, it was going to be a waiting game.

Lily was starving. The house restaurant was closed as it was 10pm so they would have to find a little bar that was still open. They only had to walk for ten minutes until they came across one that was packed with people. After they ordered, Reece went to the bar to order a bottle of wine for their table. He felt they had something special to celebrate tonight. As he sat across from Lily, this took him back to their quiz days when they were lovers. How he wished it was still like that, but so much water had gone under the bridge since then and he realised he had lost it all. He reached across and held her hand. Lily did not withdraw her hand; this was all about their daughter, and they were both over the moon.

Reece chatted on. He was so happy he now knew where their daughter was. She was alive and for so many years he had given up, thinking the worst. As they ate their dinner the atmosphere was one of both sadness and happiness, depending on who they were focusing on. He was still angry with Amelia for all her lies and now to find out she had stolen his daughter and left him to suffer, she would never be forgiven. But why would she have done that; would they ever know? The only good to come from Lily's findings was the fact that Leila was doted on and loved; Amelia had been a good mother to her. But the sadness Leila had endured throughout her young life was immeasurable, especially the rape, which was what upset Lily the most. They didn't know much about it, as they had only heard half the story, but how did Leila cope? Was the little girl the product of that horrible experience?

As they walked back to the resort, Reece reached out

and took Lily's hand. Again, she didn't protest, she knew he was happy and she didn't want to dampen his feelings. When it came time to say goodnight at her door, Reece asked if they could have a coffee together. It was here he wanted to know if tomorrow they could start looking for Leila. When it was time for him to go, Lily walked to the door with him, where he took her in his arms and kissed her. "I love still you, Lily. Please can I stay with you tonight so we can talk? I don't want today to end; this is the happiest I have been in many years."

Lily thought on this, perhaps he did deserve a little of her time, so they sprawled out on the bed together and talked on what might eventuate. Lily listened to Reece prattling on, but tiredness got the best of her and she dropped off to sleep. Reece pulled the bedclothes over her then cuddled into her, pretending they were both lovers again.

When Lily woke, she was surprised to find Reece lying next to her. They were both under the bedclothes but still fully dressed. She knew nothing had happened, and she was not the least bit interested in him in a sexual way, but to Reece there was still hope.

They both laughed at their situation. Lily thought the best place to start today would be to wait outside the university's main entrance and watch for Leila. All they had as a reference was the photo Reece had taken at Sea World, while they were watching the dolphin display.

<h1 style="text-align:center">Amelia's letter</h1>

L eila had plucked up the courage to let Mitchell take her to see her mother's solicitor. When they arrived, he suggested he would stay in the car as these were personal matters that would be discussed, but she begged him to come with her. He knew in his own mind that truths were going to be uncovered and wondered how she would deal with them, if he wasn't there for her, as she was still very fragile. He heard her calling out at night in her sleep, having nightmares, and she even walked the floor in the dead of the night. How he wished he could take her in his arms and comfort her, but this would be breaking her trust.

Leila and Mitchell were sitting opposite Mr Jarrad, the solicitor, at a rather large boardroom desk, where he had papers spread out in front of him. "I wish we had met under more pleasant circumstances, Leila. Until my talk with Mitchell, I certainly didn't associate these recent murders with any of my clients. I have read your mother's will and you are the sole beneficiary. She said she had written two letters to be given out on her death, the one to you had to be delivered personally by me and the one to New Zealand had to be registered, so I have sent it off. Do you have any questions to ask me?"

"Why would Mother be writing to someone in New Zealand? We don't have any ties there," she asked.

"But you and your mother came to Australia when you were about six years old. Do you not remember living over there?"

Leila looked startled. No, Amelia had not mentioned about them living in New Zealand. "I thought I was born here in Australia, am I not an Australian citizen?"

The solicitor told her she had a New Zealand passport, and that in fact she was a Kiwi. She looked at Mitchell in bewilderment. She naturally thought for all her years she was an Australian. "I cannot believe Amelia never told me. Why would she hide that from me?"

Mitchell wondered if there were more surprises to come, and how strong was she going to be. All he could do was to be there to support her.

As they drove out to the acreage Leila was very quiet, so Mitchell left her to her thoughts. He did wonder what surprises would be in the letter she was clutching in her hand. When they arrived, she climbed out of the car and went inside and curled up on the settee. Mitchell told her to sit and read the letter, and he would prepare their tea. From the kitchen he could hear, "Oh no," then "Oh my

God. Mitchell, come here,' so he hurried through to the lounge. There curled up in a ball sat Leila, tears falling from her eyes, and the letter was clasped tightly in her hands which were shaking uncontrollably.

"What is wrong, Leila?"

There was silence then more tears. "I don't know where to start. I'm not who I thought I was. Amelia stole me from a family when I was about six years old. All these years I have lived a lie, but she did love me, and I loved her, I know that in my heart. But why steal me from my family? They must have been devastated. I wonder if they still remember me? Is that why she wrote to someone in New Zealand, to say she was sorry? I wonder who I really am?"

Mitchell sat beside her and took her hand in his. "Just think about this, Leila. You have had so much to deal with lately. Put this on the back burner until you have fully recovered from your losses. I will help you; I want to become involved," he spoke gently to her.

"But you are involved. How would I have gotten through all this without you?" she told him.

A pang of sadness overcame Mitchell, for if not for his father's philandering ways, he would never have met her, but what circumstances to meet under. It was times like this he wished his father had died many years before, as his mother had a hard life and when it became too much for her, she bailed out. He knew about his father's wandering ways, as it was a topic he heard much about at home, in his younger life. He felt hurt and embarrassed when he learned of the huge age difference between him and Leila's daughter, Willow, and to think Leila was younger than himself, it didn't bear thinking about. Would he always carry this on his shoulders, the disgrace his father brought upon him? Whenever he looked at Leila it was a sad reminder of what had happened to her, to have her innocence stolen by a man old enough to be her father. He wondered if she had blocked it from her mind. Perhaps one day she might talk to him about what happened.

Mitchell left Leila to carry on reading her letter while he cooked their tea. She couldn't believe what she was reading: she had a half-sister and brother who were twins. Her father was married to her mother; they parted after the twins were born to the new partner. Her mother was a lawyer and her father a hotel manager. Amelia only found them when her father died and Leila's mother handled his estate. It was then she found her own half-brothers Reece and Kennedy, her only living relatives, until then she had no one. She was made welcome into this new family. It was then she got to know their children, and she and Leila had a special bond. She knew she would never marry so saw this as an opportunity to have her own little girl. She stole her at Auckland Airport and departed the same day for Australia. She was sorry for the heartache she bestowed on these two families, but it was a means to an end for her, to give Leila the love that she never knew.

She craved to have a little girl who she could protect and love and to keep away from the horrors that some people suffered, including herself. She wanted to be the mother she never had, so when the opportunity came, she took it.

Leila pondered over all this. What horrors had Amelia encountered? She had never spoken of them. Then she thought of something that was missing: there was no mention of the opposite sex and when she had mentioned to Amelia that perhaps she could find a partner, the subject was always sidestepped. Was this a clue to what Amelia mentioned in the letter, and why she had suffered? She continued reading: 'I am sorry Leila you had to learn all this, you brought so much joy to my life. I loved you completely. When Willow came along, it was a new journey for me, as I never had you as a baby. Thank you, my darlings, for helping to repair my life. You both gave me hope and faith that I thought I had lost forever. Love in its right context is beautiful and you both gave me that. Forgive me my darlings. Yours forever, Amelia.'

The end of Amelia's letter brought heartfelt tears. Leila was mentally exhausted; all the strength ebbed from her body, which left her feeling completely empty. Who was she, who did she really belong to? At this moment she didn't know if she loved or hated Amelia for what she had done. Her head was all over the place, but in the face of it all, she knew she loved Amelia and she was loved in return.

Mitchell called her to come and eat as he had plated up dinner. She walked through to the dining room where the table was set and her meal was on the table. Before Leila sat down, she walked over to Mitchell and hugged him, telling him he was her rock and she didn't know what she would have done without him. This was music to his ears. If only he could tell her about his feelings, but he realised this situation was more complicated than most. In fact, in legal terms, would any attachment between them be allowed? This was something he would have to look into. Legally, could they ever become husband and wife?

Their dinner was eaten in silence, as Mitchell wanted Leila to bring the conversation to him when she was ready. He could see she was deep in thought, perhaps still trying to absorb all she had read in Amelia's letter. He would leave it up to her to talk, when she felt the time was right.

Leila helped him clear away the dishes, then excused herself as she wanted to go to her room for time out to reminisce. Mitchell watched her as she left the room. She stopped off in the lounge and picked up her letter and headed to her room. She wanted to curl up in her bed with the letter and read it through again, just to reassure herself that Amelia loved her for all the right reasons. She couldn't fault her as a mother, and they loved each other, but the big question was why did she steal her from another family and what heartache did it cause them? Leila couldn't for the life of her imagine the sorrow that family had suffered. Again, the mention in her letter of the heartache that Amelia had suffered, if perhaps Leila knew what it was, might have explained why this had all taken place.

As she lay there, a memory came flooding back: why was Amelia so upset when she knew she had spoken to a man during a visit to Sea World, especially when it was mentioned he was from New Zealand? She remembered he asked to take a photo, but she refused. Who was this man? Did he think he knew her, or was he searching for her? It was only when they went to the photo shop to get photos printed of Willow's day at the beach that the girl behind the counter told them he was visiting from New Zealand. He showed her a photo he had taken at the dolphin display in which Leila and Willow were in the background, so he asked if she knew where she lived. As Leila tried to recall more of that day it drew a blank.

As she read the letter again, she couldn't believe her mother was a lawyer, as that's what she was studying herself. Was this coincidence, or was it a gene that had been passed on to her? A warm feeling passed through her body; it was the only warmth that came from the letter. What Leila had to tell herself was all this was her past life; now she had to begin a new one. For a moment her thoughts switched to Willow, how she had been afraid she could never explain to her about her father, if she had ever asked, but now she had been spared that embarrassment. Sometimes when she had looked at her, sad memories would flood her mind, but she kept these feelings to herself. It wasn't what she went through during that time, as she was drugged so knew or felt nothing, it was not knowing what actually happened when she woke up. It was the embarrassment she felt for months that was the pinnacle of her suffering.

It wasn't until many months later, until the perpetrator's death, that the identity of Willow's father had been revealed. A relationship of trust had been broken in the worst possible way! It was all too much. Leila closed her eyes and dropped off to sleep.

She woke to a knock on her bedroom door. "Are you awake, Leila? Is everything okay? You will be late for class," Mitchell reminded her.

"I'm coming," she called to him. She jumped out of bed. No time for a shower she told herself, as she hurriedly dressed. Leila ran to the kitchen where there was a piece of toast buttered for her.

"Grab your breakfast," Mitchell called. "I'll go and start the car."

As Mitchell let Leila out at the entrance to the university, he asked what time she wanted to be picked up. "I'll be ready about 3.45. Thanks a million, big brother, I will see you then."

He watched her as she entered the building. She seemed a little happier today. But he was disappointed about the 'big brother' expression; was that the way she thought of him? His feelings were way beyond that, but he had to give it time, as she had a lot to get through yet. Today he was going to surprise her and put up some of her family photos, as he felt the time was right. They were still in boxes in the spare room. He looked at focal points to hang them so if they were seated at the dining room table, they would be able to talk about and admire them. Leila had sort of forgotten about them, and he didn't know if that was intentional, or just that she hadn't got around to thinking about it. No doubt he would find out tonight when she came home.

Reece and Lily decided to wait in their hire car outside

the university entrance, to see if they could spot Leila. It was a long shot but one worth taking. They had no idea of any class times, but it didn't matter. They would wait to the end of time, if that's what it took to get their daughter back. They had brought their lunch to eat in the car, while waiting in anticipation. The time ticked by slowly, but about 3pm students started leaving the building, so their eyes were on spotting duty. A lonely figure caught Lily's eyes as she made her way from the building. She looked at her watch then made her way to a seat where she sat down.

"Look, Reece, does that look like our Leila?" she asked.

He strained to see. "Yes, that's the girl I spoke with at Sea World that day, that's her, Lily. What do we do?"

As Lily was thinking, a young man approached the lonely figure, and they both walked towards a car that was parked just ahead of them. They decided to follow them to see where they were going. They followed the car as it headed to the outskirts of town towards the countryside. A couple of kilometres later it pulled off into a long driveway, so Reece slowed down and saw it pull up in front of a large home. They watched as the two people entered the home together.

"It looks like Leila has a partner. Thank God she hasn't gone through this on her own," sighed Lily.

Reece could see tears welling up in her eyes; she was still the doting mother, worrying about her daughter.

"You know, Reece, I can still remember the last words she said to me, 'Don't cry, Mummy, I'm just going to have a holiday with Daddy.'" That was the end: Lily couldn't hold back. She just had to let out all her emotions. All those years had passed, and now they had Leila back.

Reece reached over and took her hands in his. "Cry as much as you like, my darling, we have our Leila back. Thank God it is nearly over. Let us go back to the resort and talk about tomorrow."

Kennedy was missing Lily, as this was the first time they had been apart for any length of time, so he was thankful he had Mackenzie and Harrison for company. They were ecstatic to know Leila had been found but saddened by what she had been through. They couldn't remember anything about Amelia, as they were only three years old when Leila went missing. But they still felt angry with her for taking Leila away. It was Kennedy who was bitterly disappointed with Amelia, as he had a soft spot for her and hoped the reunited family members would remain lifelong friends, but now that friendship had come to a sad end. He could not understand the logic of her stealing Leila, knowing it would cause much heartache among the families, especially when they had made her so welcome. Instead, she had hoodwinked them into believing she had met a man online and a romance had begun, and that was her reason for going to Australia. So many lies were told over the years, but not for one moment did they think of her as the perpetrator; it just didn't enter their minds.

A letter arrived in the post addressed to 'Kennedy, Lily, Reece' care of Kennedy's address. He noticed the letterhead, from a solicitor's office on the Gold Coast, which he thought most strange. He slipped his letter opener into the envelope and was surprised to find a handwritten letter from Amelia. Before he started to read, a little note fell out of the letter and it was from a Mr Jarrad, Amelia's solicitor, explaining he was to send this upon Amelia's death. Kennedy sat down to begin reading.

What lay before him was a heartfelt letter, starting from Amelia's life as a child. How after her mother had walked out, her twin brother Peter had tragically died, so there was only her and her father left. She became his possession, thus leading to sexual abuse from a young age, and the only way out of this tangled web was to leave home, which she did the day she turned sixteen. Apart from her father trying to persuade her to come back to him several times, she changed jobs, and never saw him until she was contacted by a hospital to say he was dying. It was then she learned he had amassed a fortune and she was the sole beneficiary of his estate.

She was scarred for life by her father's abuse, so no other man was ever going to be allowed to touch her. She longed to have a daughter that she could love and be loved in return. When she and Leila formed a loving bond, this was her one chance to become the loving mother she had longed to be, so she took that opportunity. She apologised for the anger and the agony she had caused her family, but for her, her lifelong dream had been fulfilled and she had loved Leila completely. Then when Leila became the victim of rape, it broke her heart and she blamed herself. But when they found out it was her surf lifesaving mentor, someone old enough to be her father, it brought back to Amelia the nightmares that she thought had gone forever. She thanked the Lord that Leila knew nothing of what happened because she had been drugged and didn't have to go through the hell that she herself had suffered.

Then came Willow, the product of this rape, but it was another chance for Amelia to be the mother figure once again. She never had Leila as a baby, so this was a wonderful experience full of love and admiration.

At this stage Kennedy couldn't hold back his tears. Not for one moment had he thought Amelia's life had been so sad. When he regained his composure, he continued reading, and this was the heartbreaking end to her letter: 'For all the pain I have caused, I love you all, so thank you for your beautiful little girl, Leila. One day she will come back to you as I have left her a letter explaining what I did. I knew she was only ever on loan to me. I beg for your forgiveness. Forever, Amelia.'

Suddenly Kennedy felt a numbness take over his body. Their loss was Amelia's gain, but for all the right reasons. How could he carry the hatred he had; it had to be let go. Leila never suffered and she was loved completely by Amelia. He was only sad that they never knew of the suffering she had put up with in her life, as they may have been able to help her. The anger in Kennedy's belly was redirected to her father, who had caused her to live in fear of men and robbed her of the right to be a loving mother in a more conventional way.

Kennedy knew when he met Amelia that he felt a closeness and that is why he stressed throughout that they never lose touch with each other. He hoped the other family members would find it in their hearts to forgive her after they had read her letter. It didn't mean what she did was right, but nevertheless they couldn't go back; they had to move forward. Amelia was no longer part of their lives in person, but in memories, good or bad, and either way she would always be present.

When Mackenzie came home from varsity, Kennedy asked her to sit and read a letter that had arrived. He wanted to see her reaction. As she began reading, tears came to her eyes. She found it hard to comprehend that such suffering existed in families, when reading about the abuse. As she read on, an understanding was forming as to why Amelia stole Leila. It wasn't right, but it must have helped her find love in her heart that she wanted to share.

"Oh, Father, how sad for her. I hated her for the heartache she caused Mother, but how could you hate someone for the suffering they themselves had gone through? How lovely she was able to find the love she so desired to give. We have lived our lives without Leila and now that we know the truth, it's not so sad. She will come back to us, but sadly Amelia's life was cut short by that terrible murder, but she has Willow to care for in heaven, and they will be together."

Kennedy hugged his daughter. She, like him, could see there was forgiveness among the heartache.

"You know, Father, no one is a winner in all this. Our sadness was Amelia's happiness but now that has ended in the most tragic way."

Kennedy had a meeting with Lincoln, as decisions had to be made on the shares in Lincoln's company's gaming proposal. His company now knew how many shares were up for grabs and because he had put a hold on them, they had to be finalised today. As Reece was still in Australia they would have to act on his behalf. Lincoln knew the worth of the shares and once they registered on the share market, the price would skyrocket. Kennedy's reliance on Lincoln to make them a healthy profit was critical, especially as they were propping up Reece, as he didn't have the same equity as himself and Lincoln. Sometimes friends involved in business together could end badly if things went wrong, but the lads had never let each other down in the business realm, although that could not be said of their personal circumstances!

Lincoln had played a big part in the programming of the computer software for this new game, and his company had onsold it to a well-known player in the gaming industry for an undisclosed figure, to which Lincoln was privy. But this information had to stay within the company's shareholders, so his partners knew nothing about it. When it came to withdrawing the large amount from their crypto wallet, Kennedy felt he had to ask, "Are you sure we are doing the right thing?"

Lincoln just smiled and gave him a wink. "Wait a week

or two and we will have reached our dream goal, of joining the billion-dollar club."

Insider information was handy in the business world, and this was how millionaires and the like stay at the top of their game, as they too are privy to insider information. This was out of the reach of ordinary people; it was the privileged few who were able to obtain information within the world of high finance.

Lincoln's company, with him at the helm, had done a copy-paste job of an old game, which was immensely popular, and had also secured the copyright. They introduced new characters and updated maps, bringing it to a high level of shine. The update incorporated events that were happening in the real world between opposing countries. With the revamp it would bring a deep experience that would monopolise all a player's spare time. This action-packed game had strayed remarkably little from its roots. Players would wander around the demon-blighted fantasy lands, with chosen characters running amuck with favourite weapons from arsenals of choice. All trying to kill the predator or enemy in their wake. The internet was already full of people doing outrageous things, with their clever little characters.

With the knowledge fed to them by Harrison, Lincoln knew there were always online friends that could be picked up at any time, day or night, for just one more mission, which put bedtimes later than planned or intended. It had become a passion that put gamers at risk of withdrawing from the outside world and from those who didn't seek their thrills in technology.

Selling this new exciting game to a reputable gaming client was the deal that would see the share prices skyrocket when it hit the share market. No one knew of this deal; it was all pretty hush-hush as it was going to take the gaming world by surprise. All the current shareholders would receive an ongoing dividend and knowing the vast number of players worldwide, the profits were unimaginable. Lincoln's excitement was hard to hide, but the minute it was lodged on the Wall Street share register, he could tell Kennedy. Then it would be a matter of how many shares they would sell and what they would keep. This would be an individual decision by each person.

Amid all the excitement of the meeting, Kennedy had not had time to tell Lincoln about the letter he had received. Not even Lily or Reece knew, so he would wait until they came home, then let them read it for themselves. Now it was time to bring Lincoln up to date on all the dramas going on in his life. As Kennedy was relaying it all to his friend, he couldn't hide the odd stray tear that didn't want to stay hidden, and being the emotional guy that he was, didn't help the cause. When he read the part on Amelia's young life and of Leila's rape, again a silence fell upon Kennedy; it was difficult even reading it a second time. Lincoln was clearly upset, and he stood up and hugged Kennedy, offering his sympathy. His stray tears turned into a flood. How he wished Lily was here to comfort him, but receiving the affection from Lincoln was the next best thing.

Kennedy woke the next morning to a phone call from

Lily, who sounded excited. "Guess what, my darling. We have found Leila. We waited outside the university then saw her being met by a young man, so Reece and I followed them in our car to an acreage, where they drove down a lane then went into the home together. We are not sure what to do now."

Kennedy told her to be careful, not to rush things as he thought back to the letter from Amelia. She said she had left a letter for Leila explaining what had happened, but as yet Lily and Reece knew nothing of this. "Perhaps if you knock, introduce yourselves and ask if you could come in and talk with her. Tell her you are related to Amelia. I don't know where it will go from there, but you know what to do, Lily. It is part of your job; you handle delicate situations every day."

Lily loved the way Kennedy put any situation at ease. "I miss you, my love, but we are almost there. Reece only has one day left before returning to work. I will stay on for a couple of days if things work out okay. Love to the twins, I will ring you tomorrow."

Today was the day Lincoln's company shares, which were onsold, were registered on the share register at the stock exchange under a well-known gaming brand. Lincoln had not given Kennedy the prospectus, which summarised the key information about the offering. He had done all the work checking behind the scenes with the new company. Once approved they could start trading the shares on the market, providing it maintained certain ongoing requirements, filing reports, holding annual meetings and complying with corporate governance rules.

Now all they had to do was wait until the share prices took their expected hike.

On day one the shares rose significantly, but it was day three that saw them skyrocket to a record price. This was cause for excitement. Would they climb higher, or would they plateau out? There were handshakes all round. Their crypto wallet would extend its worth, but first they had to make decisions as to how many shares to sell and how many to keep. Reece would be in for a big surprise when he next met with the lads.

The wait for Leila

J ust as they did yesterday, Reece and Lily sat outside the university entrance waiting on Leila to come out. She didn't disappoint and at 3.30pm there she was, but this time she was on her own. She made her way to her car and drove off. Reece followed, hoping she was heading back to yesterday's destination. That was exactly what happened and on her arrival at the lane she drove up to the home.

"What say we call on her now?" suggested Reece.

Lily thought on this for a minute. "Yes, now is the time. Drive up to the home, Reece, and we will see how we handle this. I am frightened as well as excited, but we must keep our cool."

He headed up the driveway and parked at the front entrance. He reached for Lily's hand and squeezed it tight. For all those years of waiting, was this the reward they so deserved? "Lily, what will we say? I'm so nervous. All I want to do is hug her."

Lily told him to let her handle the situation, not to rush Leila, just let it play out.

As Lily was about to knock on the front door, a man appeared from behind them. "Can I help you?" he asked.

This startled Reece and Lily. "We would like to speak with Leila," replied Lily.

"I'm Mitchell, Leila's friend, do come in."

They followed him into the lounge. "Leila, you have visitors," he called as he offered for them to sit down. Lily's heart was racing. How was this going to play out, could she contain herself enough, so as not to act impulsively? As she looked around, there was a photo of Amelia, Leila and presumably Willow, so she got up and walked over to the photo. She lifted her hand and touched the little girl. Next thing someone was standing beside her.

"That is my daughter, Willow."

Lily spun around and apologised. "Hello, I'm Lily and this is Reece," and before she could say any more Leila interrupted, "I know you," she said as she looked at Reece. "I met you at Sea World a few weeks back. Who are you? Do you know me?" she asked. Reece sat stunned. What could he say? But it was Lily who spoke. "Amelia was our half-sister from New Zealand. I don't know how to say this to you, Leila, but Reece is your father and I am your mother. Amelia took you from us when you were six years old. Not a day has passed that we didn't miss you. We love you, Leila, You are our daughter."

Leila stood rigid like a statue. So these are the people Amelia talked about in her letter, who she was stolen from.

Lily spoke again. "We know you have been through the most traumatic time, Leila, and this is another shock for you, but please believe me when I tell you we love you dearly. Please can I hug you? It seems like an eternity since you left us."

With this, Leila came forward and Lily welcomed her into her arms. They clung to each other, and the tears flowed.

Mitchell watched all this unfolding. What lovely people, he thought to himself. He was saddened to hear of Leila being taken away from them. He had not met Amelia as tragically she was taken along with Willow before they had a chance to meet, and here were two people who had lost a daughter and wanted her back. Reece stood up and went over to join Lily and Amelia. He now had his daughter, his only child, back, making his world rosy once again, apart from one last thing – he also wanted his Lily. Lily withdrew and let Reece hug his daughter. She went across to Mitchell and asked him how he and Leila met; was it through the university? How was he going to answer this? It was his worst nightmare that plagued him each day and here it was again. Leila heard this question and interrupted, "We met through mutual friends." Lily could see this was an uncomfortable moment, so asked if they could sit down.

"Please feel you can ask us any questions you like," she told Leila. Leila looked at Reece and Lily. Here were her biological parents; what did she want to know? "Amelia left a letter with her solicitor to give to me upon her passing, and she explained what she had done. I was shocked, but she was a great mother, and she loved Willow and me." This was the first real reference to the little girl, so Lily walked over to the photo and touched Willow. "What a beautiful little girl," she said.

Tears appeared in Leila's eyes, "Yes, that photo was taken one day we went to the beach, and she threw sand in the air and it all came down and landed in her hair. In fact, when we dropped the camera into the photo shop to get the photos printed, the assistant, a girl I knew, told me that a man had a photo of me and asked if she knew where I lived. She said he was from New Zealand. I remembered you, Reece, and did wonder who you were.

Reece told her he had flown back to the Gold Coast hoping to meet her again, and he had spent two days at Sea World waiting for her to return, "But sadly you never turned up, so I went back to the photo shop to speak with the young assistant, but she had moved on." He explained how they had a forensic artist draw up an image of how she would look today and it was a near match to the person in the photo. "That is when our searching began. Before that it was classed as a cold case in New Zealand as the police had exhausted all avenues.

"We never forgot you, Leila. We just never imagined Amelia had stolen you, as she was family."

Leila's tears just kept coming, as before her were two strangers who were her actual mother and father. Weirdly, she felt a connection to them; they didn't feel like strangers any more. "I don't know what to say or how I feel, it is so overwhelming. I have lost Amelia and I still have a mother and father."

Lily reached out for her again and within seconds they were back in each other's arms. She whispered to Leila, "You were my first born, please come back to me." All was silent as they stood and tried to take it all in. "We will leave you for now and if it is okay, could we please come back after dinner? It will give you time to talk things over with Mitchell. Reece has to return home tomorrow, but I can stay on for a couple of extra days," said Lily.

"Please do come back. I'll have thought of more questions by then," replied Leila.

Reece gave Leila a hug as they departed and said their brief goodbyes.

Back at the resort Reece and Lily hugged each other in excitement. They had held their stolen daughter and felt deep down she was receptive to them. Lily knew it wasn't going to be an easy ride, and there would be hurdles to negotiate along the way, but Reece was more upbeat. In his eyes he had his daughter back, and nothing could get in the way.

Meanwhile Lily had something on her mind that she wanted to bring up with Reece. "Did you feel in our conversation that Willow was bypassed? I am wondering if perhaps she reminded Leila of what happened to her and now that she has gone, those memories will also disappear. I am sure she loved her, but I feel sad for that little girl. But then I put myself in that position, how would I feel?" Suddenly a little of Lily's past came flashing back to her. She knew what it was like to be taken without consent, but now Kennedy, the perpetrator, was the love of her life. She wondered what Leila had experienced and what she had remembered. "I would like to talk with Leila about what happened. Perhaps Mitchell might be able to throw some light on it. I don't know if they are partners or just good friends, but obviously he owns the property. Really, we don't know much at all, so hopefully that will change when we go back later."

As Reece looked at Lily, feelings from days gone by were resurfacing. He still loved her, she was the mother of their daughter, they had gone through so much now and he wanted her back. He still blamed Kennedy for taking her away from him, but he knew deep down he had his chance, and he blew it. Could they rekindle their love? He hoped so. With Leila back on the scene, perhaps this was the beginning. He thought over what Lily had said about Willow, and, yes, he agreed, it was as if she was just a shadow.

As they knocked on Leila's door for the second time today, both Leila and Mitchell came to greet them, followed by hugs all round. There was an awkward moment until they were all seated then Reece spoke. "This is a lovely home, Mitchell; do you own it? What is the nature of your work?" This was going to take a lot of explaining. First, he would tell of his career. "I have just come home from Canada having completed my degree as a forensic scientist. I never met Amelia or Willow as I returned the day the tragedy happened. Leila never arrived, as was arranged, to pick me up from the airport.

Our solicitor picked me up instead and it was from him that I learned that Leila was in hospital." Lily picked up on this: Mitchell and Leila mustn't have known each other very long. She didn't want to cause any embarrassment so let it pass.

Now Mitchell had to explain the home situation. This could be a problematic one, he thought. "Actually, Leila and I are joint owners of this property," he told them.

"Let us move on from here," suggested Leila. "I believe you are a lawyer, Lily. I'm studying law myself."

Lily told them she was now a High Court judge and was thrilled that she had followed in her footsteps, taking on law. "What made you interested in law?" she asked. There was a slight hesitation before she answered. "I want to protect vulnerable young girls and women against male predators, who are lurking out there in society," then she stopped short and looked at Mitchell and apologised. He signalled that all was fine. This mystified both Lily and Reece. Why did she apologise for what she said? It really didn't have anything to do with Mitchell, surely. Again, an awkward silence fell over the room. It was Lily who spoke first. "Did you know you have a half-brother and sister? They are twins, Mackenzie and Harrison, and they are nineteen years old. They can't wait to meet you. They didn't remember much as they were only three when you went missing. Reece and I parted; I am living with Kennedy who is the twin's father. I met Amelia through handling her father's estate, as he was a very wealthy man, but I never met him. She asked me to help find her mother, as she walked out on them when they were six years old. It was only then we found out she had several other partners that she had walked out on, leaving children behind. Amelia turned out to be Reece and Kennedy's half-sister. Lily explained that it was a complicated situation, as the three of them shared the same mother but had different fathers. It took Leila a minute or two to take all this in.

"I often wondered why Amelia never had to go to work as there was always money available. Now I am finding a little of her background, as she never discussed her past life. Was she an only child?" she asked.

Reece explained she was a twin, but her brother Peter died at age six or thereabouts. Her mother left her twins and moved on. She had done this to Kennedy's family previously, and before that she had a child out of wedlock. "It appears all Amelia had was her father. Other than that, we are in the dark!"

Leila was starting to put together a picture, but one point eluded her, "She mentioned in her letter that she had faced horrors of her own. Do you know what they might have been?" Neither Reece nor Lily could answer this question, as they knew nothing beyond their first meeting.

Reece wanted to know more about Leila's ownership in the property. "Did you buy half the property out of your inheritance?"

"No, the estate money has not been disbursed as yet. Truth be known, it was left to Willow..." Then she stopped suddenly, realising what she had said.

Reece apologised as he didn't want to cause any

embarrassment. "Where are we going to go from here?" he asked. "Would you consider coming home to New Zealand to be with your family?"

This came as a complete surprise to Leila, as she considered Australia to be her homeland. "It is too early for decisions to be made, as I have Mitchell and our property as well as university to consider. I need time to put my life together again, as I am still recovering from my losses. Mitchell has been a strong support for me. I don't know how I would have coped without him. He came on the scene as this tragedy unfolded. When I woke from the shock of it all, a couple of days later, he was sitting at my bedside, a total stranger who I had never met before, but I knew of."

Reece and Lily looked at each other: if they were total strangers, why was he at her bedside, who was he and what did he mean to Leila? They couldn't put their finger on the tie-up between the two of them.

Reece told Leila he had to fly out tomorrow. He would love to stay, but he had taken a lot of time off work lately, all in pursuit of finding her. "I don't want to leave as I feel we have so much more to talk about. I love you, Leila, you are my only child and I want you to come back and be part of our family again. Please give this some careful thought as we have missed all those years together. We will never get the past back, but we can build a future as a family." With these words he went to her and held her in his arms. Tears flowed as he begged her to come home to him.

Lily looked on; tears appeared as she could see at that

moment how much Reece missed his daughter. As she thought back, she missed her too, but she had Mackenzie and Harrison to take her mind away from the suffering, while he had no one.

Leila took all this heartache in, and it tore at her heart. "I will have a serious think on where my life is going. At the moment there are clouds coming and going and until there is a clearing, I can't make any decisions. Please allow me time," she begged.

On this note final goodbyes were said to Reece, as this was his last moment for now with his daughter. Lily told Leila she would wait a day before she came again to visit, as this would give her time out to think.

Back at the resort, Reece brought up with Lily about Leila and Mitchell being total strangers at the time of the tragedy, but that was only a couple of months ago, so what was the tie-up, why were they sharing a home? Then there was the property: how could it be left to Willow? She was just a child. There were so many questions needing answers, but as they had just met, now was the wrong time. Lily told Reece she would try to find out more on her next visit. "Did you see signs of them being more than just friends?" she asked. Reece had noticed that Mitchell came across as a protective partner, but he hadn't seen any physical signs between them. Perhaps Leila was not ready for a relationship, as her suffering was still raw.

"Things don't seem to add up and I can't put my hands on why. Do you think she will come home to us, Lily?" he asked. "I would love to think she can begin to love us enough to break ties with Australia, but her loved ones are buried here and then there's Mitchell. Does he have a hold over her? I don't know where this is going, but we can only live in hope that one day she will belong to us again." These words brought tears from Reece. What Lily had said didn't seem convincing enough to him. He had hoped for a more positive outcome, but at this moment there wasn't one.

This morning Lily hugged Reece goodbye as he was boarding the shuttle for the airport. Then words flowed, words that had been bottled up in Reece's heart for the past week. "I love you, Lily. Please give me a second chance. We could be a family again when Leila comes home. We loved each other once, and we can go there again," he pleaded.

In Lily's heart she knew this could never happen. She loved Kennedy completely, and no one could take his place. "I'm sorry, Reece, we went there once and it didn't work; we can't go back. I want us to be good friends, nothing more."

After taking in these words, a dejected Reece climbed aboard the shuttle.

What will today bring, Lily asked herself as she drove out to Leila's. Leila and Mitchell were waiting for her. There were hugs again, making her feel welcomed.

"Well, I'll leave the two of you to talk as I have a job interview with the Queensland police. I will be back later," and with this farewell, Mitchell left.

"Let us walk around the garden," suggested Lily, hoping it would allow Leila to open up a little about herself. "The grounds look lovely. Who looks after them?"

she asked. Leila said that Mitchell looked after them now, but a gardener was employed by Michell's father's solicitor, while he was in Canada.

"Did you live here on your own?" Lily asked.

"Yes, I moved here to escape from the reporters and the publicity when details were leaked to the press about a surf lifesaving mentor who broke his position of trust with a teenager. And when it was linked to me, I was hounded day after day, and that's when I moved out of Amelia's home, to here."

"Oh Leila. I'm so sorry you were put through all this; can I ask what happened?" Lily was hoping she had won Leila's trust. Leila felt she could talk to Lily so told her the whole story about her rape. "I don't know what happened because I was drugged so the only recollection was waking up in a boatshed on the beach. Months went by and still I didn't know who did this to me then when I found out I was pregnant I still didn't know."

"Come to me my pet, let me hold you," cried Lily. As they held each other, Leila felt the comfort she desperately needed. It wasn't the same talking to Mitchell, as she needed to feel a warmth that she had missed when she lost Amelia.

"Thank you, Lily, I'm so happy you are here," sobbed Leila. They linked arms and walked back to the home. Lily asked Leila to talk her through the photos hanging on the walls. As they passed a box full of toys, Lily asked if they were Willows. "Yes, Mitchell brought back lovely toys from Canada for his half-sister, but of course she never got to play with them." These words stuck in Lily's head, half-sister, Mitchell's half-sister, what did she mean? It took her a few minutes to work this out. If Willow was Mitchell's half-sister, then his father must have been Willow's father. Oh my God, the age difference between the two siblings must be twenty-six years, that would mean he was in his fifties, old enough to be her father. No wonder Leila wanted to become a lawyer to protect vulnerable girls. Then what was she doing here, living with the son of her rapist? Her first thoughts were to get her out. Suddenly there was a knock on the door, so Leila went to answer it.

Two police officers stood there and asked Leila if they could come in. Lily was surprised to see the officers as they came into the lounge. "Leila, we are here to talk to you in private," they said as they looked at Lily.

"It's fine. Lily is family," she said. They told her they had found the second youth connected to the murders and he was now in custody. It had taken a long time. The other youth of course was found dead in the crashed car.

"Why did they do this to my family?" sobbed Leila. The youth in custody was interrogated and he told the officers his 'old lady' worked in a fashion store in town, and he had heard her talk of this wealthy lady who bought lots of beautiful clothes and always paid cash for them. She also owned a red Ferrari, so apparently this was the motive for the robbery. They thought there would be money stored in the home, of which there apparently was.

Leila couldn't stop her anger. "Clients' details should not be discussed at home. I hope you speak to the parents."

One of the police officers said, "That's where we are going now. We are sorry that this tragedy has happened, Leila. If we can help in any way, you know where we are. We will keep you up to date on court proceedings."

Leila walked out with the officers as they left her home.

This gave Lily time to rethink Leila's situation. Here she was living with her rapist's son, which was far from ideal, in fact immoral in Lily's mind. How would she judge this decision if it was before the court? She didn't know, as she had never come across a similar situation! She hoped there was no romance happening between them. In her eyes it definitely was not right, but was it against the law? Lily had to find out from Mitchell his feelings towards Leila, before they became legally bound to anything.

When Leila came back into the room Lily asked her to come and sit beside her. "I want to ask you, Leila, how involved are you with Mitchell."

Leila hesitated. "He was the only person to help me through all this mess, so I guess I have become reliant on him. To me it is more a big brother friendship, but I think he has feelings for me. Why do you ask?"

Lily didn't want to jeopardise the bond she felt was forming between them. "Oh I just wondered. He seems a nice person." And that is where it finished.

Soon after this Mitchell arrived back from his interview. "How did it go?" asked Leila. Mitchell looked a bit despondent. "It went okay but there are a couple of issues they are looking into, but we will talk about it later. How has your afternoon gone?" he asked.

Leila told him of the police visit and why the murders had occurred. "The little criminals, fancy seeing this as a quick fix to get their hands on easy money. They were on a path of destruction, if not your family, it could have been someone else. All this was so unnecessary, and I am truly sorry that it was your loved ones," he said, then went and sat next to Leila and put his arms around her. Lily picked up on this; there were definitely feelings coming from him. What could she do? She couldn't allow it to progress into a full-on relationship. Would it be wrong in the eyes of the law? But how could she interfere without losing Leila?

Lily's instincts kicked in. She would find out Mitchell's father's name and start a search while still in Australia, as she only had a couple more days before she left to fly back to New Zealand. She didn't know what she hoped to find, but there must be something out there on him. She would start at the library, then search the papers around the date the rape took place.

Today Leila had an appointment with Amelia's solicitor and Mitchell couldn't go with her as he had another interview, so she called Lily to see if she would accompany her. One hour later she picked her up and they drove to the central business centre to Mr Jarrad's office. He was expecting them and invited them to be seated around the boardroom desk. Leila introduced Lily as a family member from New Zealand. After the pleasantries, it was down to business. "I have asked you here today to tell you the probate on your mother's will has come through, so now it can be disbursed. If you give me your bank details, I will deposit it tomorrow. You realise you are a wealthy young lady as Amelia had investments that are ongoing. I have put the relevant papers in an envelope. Read through them and come back if you want me to explain anything. As you know the home was demolished, so there was insurance. Also the section is in a very sought-after area, so it brought a good price.

"How are you and Mitchell getting along? He seems a decent young man."

"Yes, he has been very good to me," replied Leila.

"If you need advice on any money matters, feel free to call me."

Leila thanked him as she gathered up her papers, then they left his office.

Seeing they were in town, she decided to visit her and Mitchell's solicitor. Although they didn't have an appointment, she hoped he could see her for a short consultation. She wanted to find out the legality of the property, now that Willow was deceased. Mitchell wanted her to have Willow's share, but now she had money of her own she felt it only fair that the property revert to him, as it was, after all, his father's estate. And did she need the reminder?

Lily said she would wait in the car, but Leila insisted she come with her. They were in luck as the solicitor was free and agreed to see them. After the introductions he asked them to sit down. "What can I do for you, my dear?"

he asked. Leila explained she wanted to know legally what happens to Willow's share of the property now that she was deceased. With this the solicitor went to his files and pulled up the will. "The will has a 'per capita' distribution. I will explain this to you. In this case, the surviving sibling would not only inherit their own half but also the deceased sibling's half. But under the sad circumstances to which this came about, I would be disappointed if Mitchell went ahead with this. You are the one who has suffered the humiliation, so deservingly Willow's share should go to you."

Leila explained that was the way Mitchell wanted it to be, but she felt she didn't need it. The solicitor protested. "I knew Alister Letterman personally and was in total shock to hear he used his position of trust in such a despicable way. And you my dear, have suffered at his hands, so surely you are entitled to some recompense. I know Mitchell hated his father for what he did, but now he has to live with that."

Leila said she would work it out with Mitchell then come back to him.

"Take care, my dear, you are indeed a brave soul," were his final words.

'Alister Letterman' – that would be a name Lily would remember. She picked up on the fact that he was a friend of the solicitor, until this all unfolded with Leila. Perhaps she could make an appointment to see him and ask questions. Yes, this seemed to be the first place to start. She just hoped he would be willing to cooperate, as he would be discussing a client.

Leila dropped Lily back at her resort and they agreed to meet the next day.

This morning Lily was on the phone to Leila and Mitchell's solicitor. She explained that she was Leila's birth mother and she had met him yesterday. She said she was a High Court judge in New Zealand. Lily outlined what Leila had told her about the rape, and that she was disgusted to think a man in a position of trust would do that to a teenager.

The solicitor didn't have a spare appointment time, but he would talk to her over the phone. "What would you like to know?" he asked. Lily asked about Letterman's personal life, whether he was married, and what sort of man he was.

The solicitor told her he was a ladies' man, and his wife walked out when Mitchell was young because of his philandering ways. He had since found out she left the country and was now living in Queenstown in New Zealand. Her name was Sarah Letterman.

What a scoop! Lily had all the information she needed, and to think she only lived three hours from her. "Thank you so much, I am grateful for that. I am a little worried if Leila should fall for Mitchell, would he always be a reminder of what happened to her. At the start it might not be a problem but later in life it could become one. This is my big worry."

The solicitor agreed it could be a future problem, as, after all, sadly he was his son.

Reece returns home

Reece arrived home to an empty house. After being in Lily's company for the past week he found his home cold and empty. He hadn't noticed this before his time away, but now he knew how it felt to have female company again and a little love. If only he could have brought Leila home with him, his loneliness would have been over. Thank goodness Lincoln had called him and invited him to a meeting at his home tonight. It would be a chance to catch up with the lads and let them know what was happening in his life.

Once seated in their comfortable chairs in Lincoln's computer room, the conversations started. First, both Kennedy and Lincoln wanted to know first hand how he felt upon meeting Leila: was she as he imagined?

"She is a lovely young lady despite all she has gone through in the last few months. I can't believe how she is coping, but then she has her mother's determination. Lily and I were quite surprised how Leila handled losing Willow, but then I suppose she was always going to be a reminder of the nightmare that had befallen her. I can't believe that Amelia stole our daughter when we had made her so welcome."

With this Kennedy interrupted. "I have a letter here that was addressed to Lily, yourself and myself and when you read it, it might help you understand why this all happened in the first place. I haven't told Lily about it, as I want her to read it and feel what I felt when I read it. I hope you have it in your heart, Reece, to change how you feel, but I will wait and hear your thoughts, after you have read her letter." With this he handed the letter to Reece. "Lincoln and I will leave you for a few minutes to read Amelia's letter, then we will get down to business." On this note they left Reece to absorb what was in the letter. Kennedy had already explained the contents to Lincoln.

When they came back to the room, there was Reece sitting with his head in his hands, the letter had fallen from his hands and was lying on the floor. As Kennedy bent down to pick it up, Reece reached down first and snatched it up. "This is about Lily's and my daughter. We should have read this first," he shouted at Kennedy. Kennedy tried to say it was addressed to the three of them and as he was the only one at the time at the address, he felt it was okay for him to open it. Silence befell the room; the shock had hit Reece and he was confused and angry at the same time.

Kennedy couldn't help but speak. "Surely, Reece, you can see what a sad life Amelia experienced growing up as a child. No child should ever go through what she did; she was starved of love and abused by her father. No man was ever going to be part of her life, but she wanted to love someone. I'm not saying what she did was okay, but a little forgiveness must be in your heart."

It was all too much for Reece and the tears flowed. He was torn between what was okay and what was not. He did not have the same closeness or compassion as Kennedy. All he saw was 'she had stolen his daughter' and that was a crime. Kennedy still had his children so he couldn't possibly understand how angry he felt.

Lincoln interrupted and told Reece to put it aside, as he and Kennedy could discuss this further after they had talked business. On went the computer and Lincoln explained to Reece about the investment they owned shares in and how the shares would triple in price, once it was listed on the share market. "We will get dividends as the renewed version of our computer game gets known. The young ones loved the old version, and I have updated maps and invented new exciting characters and arsenals, so they can all run amuck and shoot and kill mysterious creatures, and themselves if they so choose."

Reece wanted to know how they got on to this investment. He was told it was Lincoln's company, so it was actually insider trading, but this had to stay hush-hush. Now the big question: how many shares were they going to sell? Lincoln could see the shares were going to rise further, as the popularity of the game became known, so this decision was a crucial one. "What do you think, Reece?" he asked.

"I'm in for the kill. Why don't we wait for a while and reap the benefit of the share prices rising further and picking up the dividends as well? It is a win–win situation."

Kennedy and Lincoln were surprised at his reaction, as usually he was the negative one of the group.

As Lincoln pointed out, the value in their crypto wallet had decreased, but when they added up their shares, their financial situation was beyond their wildest dreams. Again, they had hit the market on the crest of a wave. First was the cryptocurrency, then the NFTs and now the latest hot topic of virtual reality and gaming. Kennedy would ask Harrison to promote their new game among his worldwide gaming geeks, as he was a lead player in the gaming world and well known in the gaming parlours. This was one time when Kennedy wouldn't interfere with the amount of time he spent on gaming. He realised it was handy to have a son who could help promote the group's investments.

Lincoln was owed a big thank you, as he made his computer room available to Harrison and Mackenzie. They all still had to declare their present health issues before they entered his home, as he was now far removed from the outside world, and felt safe in his own environment. Even his long-time partner had been discarded. He had his avatars, and he never had to worry about their health issues! Kennedy worried that Lincoln was now totally living in the virtual world and had cut himself off from the real world. He was experiencing only three of the five senses – hearing, sight and taste – gone were touch and smell, but he seemed happy with his virtual life. When Lincoln listened to Reece and Kennedy's problems, he had no compunctions about the way he lived, as these didn't exist in his world.

Kennedy tried to explain to him that touch was the most important of all senses, without touch you lose all realisation of being close to someone. To reach out and touch someone gives feelings of intimacy or friendship. He tried telling him that touch was more than just a physical sensation; it was an emotional one as well. Did he not crave to be touched, Kennedy wondered. But then, he was the caring emotional type who loved to be touched and who loved touching. It left him wondering if perhaps Lincoln had not yet met the right person. Could he find intimacy with an avatar? If all he wanted was to be in control, then yes, perhaps this was all he needed. Kennedy was perplexed by Lincoln's way of thinking. And then there was Reece, who seemed an unemotional person. He knew this through Lily, and today when Reece read Amelia's letter, all he could think about was his loss, not a single thought towards Amelia's sad life.

The lads took a vote and they agreed to hang in for a couple of months, not to sell but reap the benefits of the share hikes and the dividends. Reece was happy to see his fortune slowly building up again. He learnt by having two relationship breakdowns, it turned out costly on his bank account. Not so much his parting with Lily as he was a scrooge and gave her little, but with Natalia it was a half of his fortune. It was only now he realised that if he had treated Lily as she deserved to be treated, he might have had a second chance of winning her back. But she let him know as he was catching the shuttle to the airport, they couldn't be any more than just friends. His heart was broken as he loved being in her company, having her to himself again. They even hugged each other, which gave him hope, but that was shattered.

As the meeting ended, Kennedy asked Reece to come to his home so they could continue discussing Amelia's letter. He agreed, so they both drove separately there. On Reece's arrival Kennedy made a cup of coffee before the discussions began. "Tell me, Reece, what did you feel in your heart, when you saw Leila again? Lily said you recognised her first at the university."

Reece said as soon as he saw her, he knew who she was, as it was her he spoke with at Sea World. "You know, Kennedy, I even spoke with Willow as she stole a chip from my pottle. I actually saw my grandchild. Sadly, Lily didn't get to meet her. I didn't get to see Amelia's home this time as I was put in jail for the night, but Lily said it was bulldozed down due to the stigma attached to it; no one would want to buy it. She spoke with a neighbour who put her straight on Amelia's life, also telling her that her daughter was living somewhere else due to being hounded by the press. I can't wait until Lily comes home."

Kennedy agreed, but not for the same reason as Reece, as he was longing to have her lying beside him so he could touch and caress her body and feel the warmth that flowed between them. He asked Reece if Leila had mentioned what had happened. "No, we never talked about that, but thank God he was deceased, otherwise I would have killed him for what he did to my daughter."

Now was the time for Kennedy to seize the moment to remind Reece that their half-sister suffered the same fate year after year, from a young child to a teenager, but to make matters worse it was her own father that was the rapist. "It makes me sick; I wish we had known when we first met her. We may have been able to help her in some way. You must feel some compassion towards Amelia knowing all this?" asked Kennedy.

Reece could not get past the fact that Amelia had stolen Leila and his loss was because of her, so, no, he was still angry with her. He had no forgiveness in his heart at all for her, as she had made his life one of suffering.

Kennedy could see Reece's attitude was never going to change, so now it was time to close on that subject.

Lily and Leila in Australia

After finding out all the information she needed on Leila's rapist, Lily would keep this to herself and not let on to Leila, as she only had two more days left with her daughter. Leila was at university during the day so that left the late afternoon and the nights to spend with her. Tonight she was hoping to talk with Mitchell and see what his intentions were, without causing a scene. She didn't know how she would react if Leila was part of his future. She would just have to wait and see. Lily had been invited for dinner so stopped off and bought a bottle of wine. Perhaps this would keep the atmosphere on track.

While Leila was in the kitchen Lily saw this as the time to talk with Mitchell. "Tell me, Mitchell, what plans do you have for your future?" she asked.

He looked a little surprised. "First, I will get a good job. This is Leila's and my home, so hopefully we will be happy here. I love her, she is such a resilient person and we have been through so much together."

This is not what Lily wanted to hear. "I was going to ask her to come back to us, to her family in New Zealand. We have missed her for all these years, and now we want her back. How do you feel about this?" Lily asked.

Mitchell looked disappointed. "But this is our home, we both own it together. I haven't told Leila I love her; I was waiting for the right moment."

Now Lily had to get serious. "I know this is not of your doing, but your father was not a nice person. Will Leila be reminded of his presence living in his home?"

This was the first reference made to his father and he was angry. "I hate my father for what he did to Leila, but I'm not him."

Lily told him she was sorry, but she felt she had to let him know she was against them living together as partners; it just didn't seem right. She asked him to keep this conversation between the two of them as she didn't want Leila upset. Mitchell agreed but was seething inside. He was already suffering from his father's reputation as the police had still not given him a clearance to join their ranks, and they were still checking his background. Now to be told by Lily that she didn't think it was proper for him to have a relationship with Leila was becoming too much for him to bear. Was his father's wrongdoing forever going to cast a shadow over his life?

His thoughts were disturbed by Leila calling for them to be seated for dinner. During their meal, Lily asked Leila if she had thought about coming to New Zealand to see what her life was like before coming to Australia and to meet her half-siblings. She said she was thinking about it, but she would have to wait until the varsity holidays, which began in a fortnight. "Would you mind, Mitchell?" she asked.

He told her it was her decision.

"By the way, Mitchell, I went and spoke with our solicitor today and by law, Willow's half of the estate reverts to you, now that she is deceased. I want you to have the property."

"But I want you to have Willow's share. You deserve it. We have had this discussion before, so why have you changed your mind?" he asked.

Leila explained now that Amelia's estate had been settled, she had her own money. The home was originally his family home so she felt it should belong to him. Mitchell saw red. "Is this because of my father, is this never going to leave me?"

Lily felt she had to intervene. "You are not responsible for your father's behaviour, but he did change Leila's life forever. Perhaps living in his home is a sad reminder of what happened." With these words Leila burst into tears. "I came here to hide from the media. It wasn't easy for me, but it was an escape. You had every reminder of your father removed from the property before I moved in and for this, I am truly grateful, Mitchell. I don't know where my life is going to take me as I'm still processing everything. Please be patient with me," she sobbed.

Mitchell's feelings for her led him to go and take her in his arms and express how he felt. "I love you, Leila. We have been through so much. I don't like to see you upset. If this home is a reminder of the past, we can sell it and start afresh."

Lily tried to look at this from both sides, but she felt there was a stigma attached to Mitchell because of his father; there shouldn't be, but there was. She certainly didn't think a relationship between them would be in the right context, as there were too many bad memories. Did Leila really love Mitchell or was it stability? Lily had experienced this with Reece, who was a stable person, but it wasn't enough in the end. It wasn't the beginning she worried about; it was what happened as the partnership progressed. If in anger, would the past be brought up? Lily told Leila there was no pressure, they all loved her, and the end decision was up to her.

Dinner ended up on a sombre note, much to Lily's disappointment. She only had one more day left in Australia and Leila had varsity until 3.30pm. Leila asked Mitchell if he would drop her off at varsity, then she would meet Lily and they would have a final meal together, just the two of them.

Lily was looking forward to spending time with Leila away from Mitchell and the property. She would pick her words carefully, as this was the last time they would have together unless she decided to come to New Zealand. This is what Lily was going to work on, as she wanted her to meet Mackenzie and Harrison and to spend time with her father as well as herself and Kennedy. She hoped this would be a turning point in her life, to take her away from the horrors she had suffered in Australia. Lily could get her into varsity in Dunedin and then let her work in her law firm.

At 3.30pm Lily was on time to pick Leila up from the university and they drove to Broadbeach where there was a great choice of eateries. They walked around the arcade until they found a quiet café where they could talk in peace. Lily ordered a cocktail which was delivered to their table. For a moment she sat and studied Leila. It was only then she noticed a likeness to Mackenzie, but of course, they were both her daughters. She had grown into a lovely-looking young woman. Obviously Amelia had given her the love that she would have given, if life had been different.

"Tell me about Amelia. Was she a good mother to you?" she asked. Leila told Lily Amelia loved her, she was her whole life, and they spent most of their time doing things together. She never bothered with men or many friends. "In fact she spoilt me but she had no one else, no other family, I was all she had. She sent me to a private girls' school where I made lots of friends. It was with them I joined the surf lifesaving club and became a lifesaver. But after I was raped, my life changed. I never went back and didn't keep in contact with anyone connected to the club.

"Amelia was angry. She wanted me to report the incident, but I couldn't as I didn't know who did this to me. It wasn't until I received a letter from the solicitor that I found out who it was, as he left half his estate to his daughter and that was Willow. This is the first time I have talked about it with anyone else other than Amelia." Tears were trickling down her cheeks. Lily put her arms around her. "Leila, you are my daughter. You can talk to me about anything, and I will always be here to listen. I can't undo the past, but I want to be your mother again. I have loved you all those years you belonged to Amelia. Please let me have that privilege."

This is what Leila needed: a shoulder to cry on and to hear she was still loved. She had missed Amelia. She had no one to hug and no one to hug her; the biggest part of her life was missing. Although she had Mitchell, it was not the same as having a mother. It was then Lily heard the words she never thought she would ever hear again.

"I feel it in my heart that you do love me, Lily. I need a mother, so please let me be your daughter."

Lily stood up and took Leila in her arms, "Those are the nicest words I have heard in a long time. We all love you, Leila. I have you back, my darling, after all those years. We must never forget Amelia; she gave you all the love you needed while growing up. Please think about coming back home to your family." There was a silence, as the words that had been spoken resonated in each other's minds. It was a golden silence that brought smiles to both women, as they felt the bond that had brought them together.

Goodbyes were sad occasions and today was no exception. Mitchell and Leila came to say goodbye to Lily before she caught the shuttle to the airport. Lily didn't want to leave Leila. She was frightened she might never see her again, now that they had only just found each other. But after yesterday's conversation she was almost convinced that when the university holidays began, she would be on the first flight to New Zealand. She hoped Mitchell wasn't going to be a stumbling block that held her back. She had his mother's name in her mind and to think she lived in Queenstown, only three hours' drive from Dunedin. As soon as she could manage, she would pay her a visit and find more about Mitchell's background. To Lily it didn't ring true that Mitchell and Leila had anything in common, especially with such degrading behaviour by his father. Was it an inherited trait? Lily knew she was putting negatives in the way, but she felt they had to be addressed.

As the shuttle pulled up, Leila came to Lily and held her tightly. It was as if she didn't want to let go. Lily whispered, "I love you, Leila. Please come home to us, my darling." And the answer she got back, "I love you, Mother," set her heart alight. Mitchell came forward with a handshake as he still had Lily's words in his mind. Tears flowed as Lily boarded the shuttle, then she heard those special words once more: "I love you, Mother."

Back home in New Zealand

Kennedy, Mackenzie and Harrison were waiting anxiously for Lily's flight to touch down. So many questions to be asked and answered. Sadly, Reece was not invited to meet Lily as no one thought of him; he would just have to wait his turn.

Once inside the terminal and all formalities had been dealt with, Lily made her way into the opening arms of her family. Kennedy let Mackenzie and Harrison be first in line, then when his turn came, he would whisper loving words, as he held her in his arms. As soon as his body came in contact with hers the chemistry was there. The adrenaline was pumping through his veins and he knew tonight she would be his completely; he couldn't wait.

The questions started flowing and Lily had to calm everyone down. One question at a time was all she could do justice to. She reached into her bag for her phone to show them the latest photos she had taken of Leila, so they could see for themselves what she looked like. This answered a lot of questions.

"When is Leila coming home?" asked Mackenzie. Lily could not give a true answer; it was a matter of wait and see. She explained the varsity holidays began in a fortnight, so until then they would have to wait unless she contacted Lily before then.

"Let us all go home and I will tell you everything," Lily told her family. Questions kept coming as they drove home. Excitement levels were high and for Lily it made her feel she was indeed missed. Kennedy told everyone he would pick up a take-away for tea so they could listen to Lily's experience. Then he remembered Amelia's letter, which he had let the twins read, as well as Reece and Lincoln, and now he felt Lily should read it.

Several hours passed as Lily relayed her findings to her family, when suddenly she realised Reece should have been in on her conversation, as she had learned a lot since he flew back home. Tomorrow she would visit him. Mackenzie and Harrison were shattered to hear of Leila's rape and the sadness she had gone through. They were annoyed with Amelia for stealing their half-sister. But the most touching was the loss of Willow, whose life had just begun when it was taken away. Lily tried to point out that as tragic as it was, she was also a constant reminder of what happened to Leila, so perhaps it was a blessing in disguise!

The one positive thing to came out of all this was a new pathway for Leila. One she was passionate about and that was to help other defenceless girls and young women, who suffered like her, to bring the perpetrators to justice. Everyone agreed on this point.

It was getting late and tiredness was setting in for Lily, so bed was suggested. She had to reserve a little energy for Kennedy, although he would be the one full of energy ready to please! She went and had a shower to help hold on to some of her strength. As she made her way to the bedroom, there on the bed lay a beautiful bunch of her favourite flowers: yellow roses. Kennedy was nowhere to be seen so she picked up the flowers to smell them when a little card fell on the bed. As she read it, her heart sang. It read, 'You are a girl with courage, a woman with a voice and a lady with class. Forever, Kennedy.' A tear of joy fell down her face, and she couldn't wait to place her hand on his heart.

As Lily climbed into bed she found a letter on her pillow, so she picked it up and started reading. Her one tear of joy turned to a stream of sad tears as she absorbed Amelia's letter. What child had to suffer as she had? It was despicable. The one parent she had left to care for her took advantage of her. Her nights became nightmares as she lay awake knowing what was going to happen next. She had no one to turn to, so suffered in silence, and with each day her hatred of men grew. She needed to be loved not used and this only stopped when she fled the family home at age sixteen.

Oh my God, thought Lily, no wonder she stole Leila. At last she had someone to care for and love, without having to have the services of a man. Forgiveness flooded her heart, and she didn't have any bad feelings for what had happened to Leila, as she knew Amelia had loved her dearly and she would have gained back her self-respect and self-esteem by sharing her love with their little girl. This must have been the pain she talked about to Leila.

As she looked up, Kennedy was standing looking at her. "Kennedy, the flowers are beautiful. Only you could have thought of this, and the card, I loved the words. You are such a romantic. I am so lucky our paths crossed in such an unconventional way that only the two of us shared together.

"When did you receive this letter?"

Kennedy said it arrived a couple of day after she left for Australia. Amelia's solicitor had been asked to send it after she was deceased. They discussed her shocking upbringing, how degraded she must have felt and the saddest thing, not being able to trust her only remaining parent, which was unforgiveable. What shame he had brought on her. "I wish we had known this when we first met her, Lily, we may have been able to help her. You would have been kind to her, in fact a trusted friend, someone who she was looking for," sighed Kennedy.

"Come to bed, my darling," begged Lily. He didn't take much encouraging, as off came his clothes and into bed he jumped. As his arms touched Lily's naked body, the adrenaline started its journey, first in his heart then down his body to his manly parts which ached with excitement and anticipation. He had great willpower and control of his body, so first it was time to touch and caress Lily's body. He knew she loved this, and it made her relax and built up an excitement that sent her into a frenzy, as her body responded to his touch. Tonight it happened all too quickly, as time away made Lily hungry for him to take her. She felt complete when their bodies were joined in love. Lily cried with joy. Oh, to have her lover back sharing her bed with her.

The next morning it was off to see Reece and let him know what happened after he left. But first Lily called into her law firm to see if all was okay. She knew her staff were competent– that's why they worked for her – and they liked and respected Lily as they saw where her work ethics had taken her … to the top! She gave them a briefing on what she had uncovered while in Australia, so chatter was rife, and many questions asked. Lily told them she would encourage Leila to come and work for her and a cheer went up from her staff.

She forgot to call Reece to see what hours he worked, so was not upset to find his door locked and his car gone. She left her card in his mailbox and would call him later. As she had time to kill, she went to the local post directory for Otago, to see if there were any phone numbers for an S. Letterman in Queenstown. It was a long shot as she may have remarried and changed her name, or she may have shifted to a new location, but Lily remained optimistic. She was delighted to find two S. Lettermans so wrote down their phone numbers and addresses. A trip to beautiful Queenstown might make a nice day's outing for her and Kennedy!

Lily only had two more days before she was required at work, for a case coming before the High Court, so now it was time to do some study. Tonight, she had the papers out when she was disturbed by her cell phone. It was getting late so she wondered who would be calling. As she listened, she heard, "Hello, Mother, I've missed you. This is Leila." Lily could have been struck down by a feather she was so excited, as this she never expected.

"Hello, my darling, this is a lovely surprise. How is everything with you?" she asked.

"I have my moments; some days are better than others. I just called to tell you I booked my flight to New Zealand today, and I arrive on the 19th. The flight is into Queenstown; is that a problem?" Leila asked.

Lily assured her nothing was a problem and asked what time the flight landed. Leila told her at 9.30pm. Everything was falling into place, as she and Kennedy would arrive early and she could look up the addresses she had written down for S Letterman. "It is so lovely to hear your voice again, Leila. We are so missing you. How is Mitchell?" She thought it courteous to ask.

Leila explained he had not been accepted into the Queensland police department and was bitterly disappointed, so he was still working out where to go next. Lily didn't ask why, but she did wonder if it was because of his father's stigma. The story had made headlines in Australia of how a young girl's mentor preyed on a vulnerable teenager who had just passed her exams to become a lifesaver. "I'm sorry to hear that, but he is young, and will pick himself up from this setback," offered Lily.

Leila said she was really worried for him. "I'm so

looking forward to coming to New Zealand to meet everyone," she added.

"Well, my darling, let's save the talk until we meet, only nine more days. I will call you before then and we will make final arrangements. Take care, my love," said a jubilant Lily.

"Bye Mother, love you all," were Leila's parting words.

If this was the one wish Lily could have, it certainly came true today, so she quietly thanked someone from above. "That was Leila, she is coming over on the 19th," she yelled to let everyone know.

"I hope she likes us," said Mackenzie.

Lily rang Reece to let him know. She hadn't caught up with him so relayed all that happened after he had left Australia.

Now Lily had to put all this excitement aside to concentrate on the case looming before the high court. She had read through the statements and could see complications ahead, but being in her position, she had to remain impartial and let it run its course. The case was embezzlement versus larceny, both punishable by law, but the difference is that embezzlement involved a breach of trust, while larceny did not. Both parties were adamant each one was right, so she knew to expect a fiery debate. Lily herself had to brush up on the differences between the two. Their respective lawyers would battle it out, but she was the final decision maker, so had to make herself familiar with the legality of both terms.

Kennedy had been at Lincoln's today as another bad

image had been flourishing in the headlines, bringing ill-repute once again to the crypto world. It all revolved around FTX which was one of the largest and most popular crypto exchange companies. The founder, in his mid-thirties, was arrested in the Bahamas and extradited to the US and pleaded not guilty to stealing billions of dollars in FTX customer deposits to fund his business and speculative venture investments, and making charitable donations and spending tens of millions of dollars on illegal campaign donations to Democrats and Republicans in an attempt to buy influence over cryptocurrency regulation in Washington. He was yet to come up for trial. This had a huge impact on the crypto market, and it didn't take much to make people write cryptocurrencies off, as a bad investment. There were always going to be rogues, as they are in every business. But for some unknown reason, any black mark against crypto hit the headlines with a vengeance.

Kennedy's firm heard news out of America that many countries were dumping the American dollar and there was talk of de-dollarisation within the Biden administration. This could reduce the economic and political power of the US, which has been using its currency as a tool to impose sanctions. So, there were big changes ahead, as there was talk of a digital dollar. This could mean a boom for the tech industry. The world was volatile and changes were on the horizon.

The lads, having first-hand information of what was happening in the business world, could make their choices before the news they were privy to reached the headlines. Countries like China were considering digital currency. It and Russia wanted to create more room for themselves to assert their interests and values in the global arena. For now, the US dollar remains the most widely used and accepted currency in the world. But for how much longer?

Lincoln could see great possibilities for the technology industry but was it too soon to make a move! There was so much going on, and no one could be sure what the future was going to look like.

Leila's arrival

L ily was hoping her court trial would be over before Leila arrived from Australia. Today was the day the trial began so there was a hive of activity in the court lobby. Lawyers were armed with their briefcases and high expectations, so now it was down to business.

As the case proceeded each day, the accusations ramped up and Lily had to decide whether it was looking towards embezzlement or larceny, and whether the perpetrator was trying to steer the judge towards the lesser charge of larceny. This all hinged on the way the said property was stolen. With larceny the property is taken from someone else without their permission and with the intention of keeping it permanently. With embezzlement the money is entrusted to someone who then uses it for their own personal benefit, without the owner's consent. So, the legality of either of these two evils can be confusing. The accused's lawyer tried to twist things out of context, while the other lawyer argued that the case before the judge was definitely embezzlement. All Lily could do was listen to the evidence from both parties then make her decision.

The trial lasted five days then the final decision was up to the High Court judge, who was Lily. Today was summons day, so after hearing all the evidence and remaining neutral throughout the proceedings, she gave the following verdict:

"Because you were entrusted with the family money, $2.5 million, which you chose to use for your own personal use without any consideration for other family members, that is considered embezzlement. I hereby convict you for embezzlement and the punishment will fit the crime. You will appear before the court on the 14th for sentencing. Thank you, ladies and gentlemen and members of the court."

Everyone stood as Lily left the courtroom. As expected, cries of protest, as well as jubilation, followed, but she was used to this; it went with the territory. Now that this case was heard, it left Lily free to prepare for Leila's arrival. She loved being in the courtroom. It was her passion and always would be, as this was her lifelong dream, and she had achieved what she set out to do.

It was the night before Leila's arrival and Reece was visiting Lily. She told him she and Kennedy would pick Leila up from the airport as they had business to attend to in Queenstown. Reece looked disappointed that he wasn't part of the equation so spoke his mind. "I think because Leila is my daughter it would be fitting for me to be there to welcome her."

Kennedy overheard the conversation and suggested, "Why don't the two of you go? She has met you both."

"No, I don't mean for you not to come," protested Reece.

It was Lily who spoke next. "That's a good idea Kennedy, as the business I have to do concerns Reece, so we can do it together."

Now that was settled, the question arose as to where Leila would stay. Of course Reece presumed she would stay with him, but as Lily explained it was a delicate situation and one perhaps better left for Leila to decide. Reece did not take too kindly to this, but it was left open for now.

Lily was all ready to go armed with her pad with the two addresses to visit. They left Dunedin early so they had plenty of time to find the two places they were looking for. Lily set the sat-nav as they approached Queenstown and the first address came up on screen as Frankton. They were nearly there, and the directions were being announced, so they listened and followed, only to end up outside a rather posh home.

Lily and Reece walked up to the door, then Lily knocked. An elderly man opened the door and asked if he could help them. Lily asked if a Mrs Sarah Letterman lived at that address. The elderly gentleman very quietly said his wife of 50 years had just passed away two weeks ago. Lily was shocked, she didn't expect to hear this. "Oh, I'm so sorry, how insensitive of me," she replied. It was then she realised this wasn't who she was looking for, as Mitchell's mother left his father about 20 years ago. With these equations not adding up Lily apologised to the man. She didn't go into any further details, so thanked him and they left.

Now it was on to the next address that Lily had put into the sat-nav. Hopefully this was going to be the one. The directions took them through the main street of Queenstown and up to the next subdivision of Fernhill. At the next turn left they had reached their destination. They were parked outside a modest-looking home where the blinds were drawn, which gave them the impression no one was home. Reece stayed in the car while Lily knocked on the door, but there was no reply. Then a neighbour came across and told Lily that Sarah was away on holiday. Lily decided to push her luck and asked if she knew if Sarah was from Australia. "Yes, she left Australia about 19 years ago after a marriage break-up and came here to live." It was then Lily knew this was the person she was after.

"Do you know when she will be back?" she asked. The neighbour said she had another three weeks. With this, Lily thanked her and said she would contact her then. With their business over they still had another six hours to fill in before Leila arrived.

Reece suggested a meal and a drink somewhere with a view so they could take in the lake. It was a lovely day and

Reece was in his element as he was with Lily, and their daughter was soon to be part of their family once again. They found a lovely place with a view. Reece went up and ordered a glass of wine and brought it back to their table. Perhaps this would mellow Lily a little. He couldn't help but say out loud what he was thinking. "This is like old times Lily, you, me and soon Leila. We had happy times together as a family, but how things changed when Leila was stolen."

Lily couldn't let this one slip by. "But, Reece, we were parted when she was stolen. You were with Natalia. Yes, we did love each other once, but sadly that all went wrong. We had different careers we both wanted to pursue and that's what came between us. Let's not go back there; we have moved forward."

"You may have moved forward Lily, but I haven't. I still wish we were together as I love you. I can't just switch off; it breaks my heart to see you and Kennedy together. I'm baffled how you changed your mind about him, as I remember you thought he was an arrogant prick," said Reece.

Lily let him know they had all changed, some for the better, some for the worse, but nothing on their parting could be blamed on Leila's disappearance. He could see the wine didn't mellow Lily's thinking after all.

They still had several hours to fill in, so they drove over to Arrowtown. Reece hoped some of the souvenir shops would still be open as he wanted to buy Leila something made of greenstone to remind her of her first day back in New Zealand, her homeland. Lily thought that was a nice gesture so offered to go halves and buy her something really nice. Luck was on their side as one souvenir shop was still open. They browsed until Lily saw a beautiful greenstone necklace with five diamonds set in a cluster on the edge of the greenstone. "That's the one I would choose," said Lily. That was good enough for Reece, so after splitting the bill, Lily passed the necklace to Reece and told him he could give it to Leila at the airport.

Time passed slowly, but suddenly there it was, the Jetstar flight was taxiing down the runway. Reece was so excited he grabbed Lily's hand and squeezed it. Here was their daughter returning to them. It would take another good half-hour before she came through customs, so they made their way to the overseas arrival area. Lily couldn't sit, she stood so she could rush up and take Leila in her arms, as soon as she cleared customs.

She had dreamt about this meeting for the past few weeks, adrenaline was rushing through her veins, as her stolen daughter was back home. But the question of how long no one knew the answer to. Lily was hoping hand on heart that she would feel part of their family. Behind in Australia she had left heartache and sad memories, except for one person and that was Mitchell. Lily wondered what hold he had on Leila. She had hoped to catch up with his mother before Leila arrived, but this didn't happen. Looking across at Reece, she could see what a huge deal this was to him, to have his daughter back. She was the one that cried every time Reece left to fly back to Auckland, always begging him not to go. Tears were a common theme back then.

Suddenly there she was coming towards them, pulling her suitcase. Lily rushed up to Leila and enclosed her in her arms. "Welcome home, Leila, it is so good to hold you again."

"It's lovely to hug you, Mother," she cried.

Meanwhile Reece took the suitcase from her, and now it was his time to hug his daughter. The tears flowed. His love for her had never left him, and she was his precious cargo. "Hello Reece, we didn't have much time together when we last met. It's nice to see you again."

He noticed she didn't call him Father. Why would that be he wondered. Hopefully that would change. "Did you have a good flight?" he asked.

Leila said she was nervous as it was the first time she had travelled on her own. "I'll go and bring the car to the door," Lily called to them. This would give father and daughter time alone.

"I have a little gift for you, Leila," Reece said, "it is from your mother and me. We want you to remember your first night back in New Zealand." He took it out of his pocket and gave it to her. She was speechless; it was so beautiful.

"This will always be special to me; it will remind me of my meeting with my mother and father on New Zealand soil."

"Would you like me to put it on for you?" he asked. Leila said she would just like to hold it for the moment. What Reece didn't realise was that she had had no man in her life for many years, so the father figure was never part of her equation.

On the drive back to Dunedin they chatted continually

as it was too dark to see outside of the car. Leila talked about her university course and how she was loving it. She was doing extra night courses so she could get her degree sooner. This was music to Lily's ears; this was definitely her daughter. She would like to have known had Leila not had that terrible experience, would this have been her chosen career. One day when the time was right, she would ask.

Reece listened on in silence, as it took him back to the time when Lily asked him to buy a share in the law firm and he refused. Now he could see perhaps that was the beginning of the end of their marriage. It was as if Lily was reading his mind.

"Did I tell you, Leila, that I have my own law firm? I employ ten staff, all qualified solicitors or lawyers." No, she didn't know but it didn't surprise her as she saw Lily as a very capable woman.

"What is it like being a High Court judge?" she asked.

It didn't take Lily long to answer. "It was my one love outside of my family. Like you, to achieve my dream, I went that extra mile, and it paid off handsomely. Anything is possible if you believe in yourself."

Leila knew at that moment why she felt a bond with Lily. They were similar in many ways. She was just finding this out as they got to know each other.

When they pulled up at Lily and Kennedy's home it was very late, 1.30am, and the home was lit up like Christmas. Everyone was there waiting to meet this special guest. Out they came, all wanting a piece of Leila.

Lily took charge, "Leila, meet your family, Mackenzie, Harrison and this is my Kennedy."

Mackenzie hugged Leila and whispered, "It is lovely to have my big sister back." Then Harrison made his presence felt. "I hope you like gaming, Sis?" he asked. This broke the ice and caused everyone to laugh. Kennedy was the last to hug Leila. His mind went back to the days when he showered her and read her bedside stories and now she was a lovely young lady. "Many years have passed, but you are still very much part of this family," he told her.

This all took a toll on Leila. They were such a welcoming family and to think she used to be part of it. How they must have missed her.

Lily could see she was overwhelmed, so suggested she go to bed and they would all catch up in the morning, which was only a few hours away.

When Leila woke, she had no idea of the time. She looked at her phone: incredibly, it was 11.30am. She dressed and made her way out to the dining room only to be met by Harrison. "Hi, Sis, did you sleep well?" he asked.

Leila looked at him and smiled.

"You will never know how much you were missed. Mother cried every day as did your father. You would cry each time he had to fly back to Auckland, begging him not to go. That's about all I remember from back then," he told her.

"It must have been really sad for them not knowing what happened to me," she replied. Harrison told her that she had been stolen at Auckland Airport and there was a blame game for a short while, but that soon was sorted out.

"What do you do, Harrison?" she asked.

"I'm a computer nerd, just like Lincoln. You will meet him soon. I'm addicted to gaming, and that's going to be my career. At the moment I am promoting a new game for Reece, Kennedy and Lincoln. It is flying off the shelves. I'll teach you to play if you want?"

Leila had very little interaction with young people her own age. That stopped when she ceased going to the surf lifesaving club. "I don't know much about gaming but, yes, it will be fun learning. Where is everyone?"

"Reece is picking you up shortly. He will take you to his home. Actually it was our family home until Mother and Reece split; that's where we all lived," he told her.

"What happened?" Leila asked.

Harrison explained as best he could about the past and present situation between Lily, Reece and Kennedy. "We all get on good together and that makes for a happy family environment," he explained.

Reece called and picked Leila up, to take her for lunch at his hotel as he wanted to show her off to his staff. "I see you are wearing your necklace," he remarked.

She told him it was so beautiful she would wear it every day. "It is a reminder of who I am and who gave it to me." With this she leaned over and touched Reece's hand.

He couldn't hold back. "I love you, Leila. You were my little girl and when you went missing my life changed forever. I was heartbroken. Remember when we met at Sea World, at that moment I felt I knew you, so I searched for a week trying to find out who you were. I even went back to Australia a second time to search as I had a photo of you. I took the photo at the dolphin performance and unbeknown to me, you and your wee girl were in the background. I took your image from house to house as you said you lived near the theme park.

He told her the rest of the story about Amelia. She was surprised that so many lies had been told, as she knew nothing, but of course she wouldn't, as Amelia's cover would have been blown. "Well, here I am today, and we have a lot of catching up to do. Thank you, Father."

These words stayed in his mind: to be called Father was his dearest wish.

All the staff at the hotel met Leila and made a fuss of her. Reece and Leila then had a nice lunch, and a bond was forming between them. After lunch Reece drove Leila to Lily's law firm to see her at her chambers. She was surprised to see her mother's name as owner on a plaque in the foyer leading into the offices. "Gosh, Mother has done well. I really like her; she is so warm and friendly. It is a shame things changed for everyone, as I would have been very happy living here."

Reece agreed that Lily was a lovely lady and Leila could see he still had feelings for her, so it was a pity their marriage didn't work out. They knocked on Lily's door and went into her chambers. She was surprised to see them, "Come in, what a lovely surprise. Come and meet my staff, Leila. They are waiting to see you." Leila was introduced to everyone and was asked if she would come and work with them one day. She replied, "I would love that."

A couple of nights later, when there was just Lily and Leila at home, Leila asked why Amelia would steal her, especially when they were a happy family. Lily decided it was time for her to read Amelia's letter as this would explain so much. She gave it to Leila and watched on intently. As Leila read what was in her hand she gasped in shock. "Oh, Mother, that must be what she was referring to when she said something sad happened in her life. Oh my God, that is terrible. She must have been so frightened. No wonder she didn't want a man in her life. Now I know why she wanted me to go to the police when I was raped. I didn't suffer from the rape because I was drugged, but it was the embarrassment afterwards that I suffered, as I had no idea who did it to me.

"I can't believe her father was such an evil man. That makes me feel really sad for her. Although she did the wrong thing, at least she had someone to love and bring a little joy into her life, and now she has gone. She and Willow will be together, so she is not alone, she won't be afraid."

These words brought tears from Lily. Leila had a soft heart not unlike herself.

Leila was fascinated when meeting Lincoln, as she had never known someone who had almost given up on the real world for the virtual world. She could see some of the things he talked about would be better done away with in the real world, but completely – no.

The days came and went and she felt part of a happy

family. For the first week she stayed at Lily's then she went to Reece's home, the family home, of which she had no memories! The three children became good friends, and she was even introduced by Harrison to the world of gaming. Lily took her to her work and she sat in on hearings, and mixed with the staff during interviews with clients, as a junior clerk. She felt this was definitely her calling.

An emergency in Australia

During her second week in New Zealand, while staying with Reece, they received a visit from the police, who asked if a Leila Hammond was staying there. Then they asked if they could come in as they had sad news. Reece sat beside Leila as they listened to what the police had to say after asking her if she knew a Mitchell Letterman. "Mr Letterman is in hospital in a serious condition. He was badly beaten then his house was set alight."

Leila burst into tears. "What happened?" she asked.

"Apparently a neighbour found out that a paedophile was living next door, so he acted. We have arrested the man and he is in custody. Mr Letterman is in a bad way. He was found unconscious in his car by another neighbour who then took him to hospital."

Reece had to control Leila as she was hysterical. "I have to go back to Australia, I have to be with Mitchell.

Oh my God, why did they do that to him?" she sobbed. "Please call the travel agent and get me a flight as soon as possible, Father. I must be there for him."

Reece told her he would contact Lily and let her know what had happened, then they would make arrangements. By this time Lily was on her way, as the police had first gone to Lily's home and asked for Leila, so Harrison then gave them Reece's address and called Lily at work. She arrived just as the police were leaving. She told them she was Leila's mother, then asked what had happened, so they explained it all to her. "The home, how damaged is it?" she asked. She was told that by the time the fire crew arrived it was totally destroyed. Oh my God, she thought, all Leila's photos of Willow would be gone, as would her memories. She thanked the police then ran inside, to find Leila in Reece's arms sobbing. "Oh, my darling, I'm so sorry. Can I do anything to help?"

"I have to go back to Australia. Will you come with me, Mother? I need you, as I have no one other than Mitchell."

Reece managed to get them seats on a flight leaving for Coolangatta the next day at 5.30pm. Lily had to make arrangements for another judge to step up in her place for a couple of weeks. Tonight turned out to be a sad occasion, as the farewells were so much earlier than anticipated. No one wanted Leila to leave, as she had just joined their family and now she was leaving. She didn't want to go either, as she realised what she had missed out on if she had not been taken from this family. But her first concern was Mitchell.

During the flight, Leila brought up Amelia's

background as she was still shocked as to what she had endured during her childhood. Then she opened up about her rape. Lily asked if she would find it hard to love a man, as curiosity had got the better of her. "Because I was drugged, I don't remember anything other than waking up in the boatshed and finding my knickers lying on the floor. More than anything, it was the embarrassment of who did this to me, so yes, I think I could physically love someone, but as yet I haven't found that person."

This was music to Lily's ears, knowing Leila and Mitchell had not made love. They talked further on Amelia's life and although she stole Leila from her family, Leila had added meaning to her life, but it was to the detriment of her own family. It was really a no-win situation.

Leila and Lily were on their way to the Gold Coast hospital to see Mitchell. When they arrived, there were police in the hospital foyer. Leila asked at reception to see Mitchell Letterman, but the police came forward and asked them to accompany them to a private room. "Do you know Mitchell Letterman? We are trying to contact his partner who is holidaying in New Zealand." Leila explained that she was his partner and had just flown in from overseas. "Is he alright?" she asked. The police explained they were trying to find out why this had happened, why anyone would want to harm him. They weren't able to give out medical information, so Leila would have to ask the hospital staff. She was told the home had been burnt to the ground, and nothing could be saved. This brought gasps from Leila. "What about my little girl's photos and Amelia's. I have nothing left, nothing, no living memories, they have all been taken from me. What am I going to do, Mother?" she cried. The police could see the distressed state she was in, so told her to go and find out about her partner.

Again, they approached reception only to be told Mr Letterman had just been taken to the operating theatre, as his condition had deteriorated. "Can I speak to someone about my partner?" Leila asked. A nurse said she would get the doctor to speak with them. Lily sat with her arms around Leila. She felt deep hurt in her heart for her daughter. She was so young to be going through so such trauma. The doctor arrived and sat beside them and explained that Mitchell was in theatre. He had a brain bleed and they were releasing some pressure. They were told he had been brutally beaten and at this early stage, his prognosis did not look good.

"When can I see him?" Leila asked. The doctor told them to go home and he would speak with them tomorrow, hopefully with better news. Lily thanked him, as Leila was sobbing her heart out.

"Thank you, Mother, I couldn't have coped on my own." Lily assured her she would always be there for her.

After finding a motel close to the hospital, they both collapsed into bed exhausted. Lily was woken during the night as Leila was sobbing and calling out. She went to her and sat on her bed, rubbing her forehead until she settled. The next morning, they called a taxi to take them to the hospital as Leila was anxious to be with Mitchell. Although it wasn't visiting hours they were taken to a ward where Mitchell was lying in a bed attached to machines. Leila leaned over him and whispered his name, but there was no response. His face was bruised and swollen, and he look like death. The nurse told them that Mitchell was put into an induced coma where he would be for a few days until things settled. "You can sit with him and hold his hand, just to let him know he is not alone," the nurse told Leila. She told Lily to go, and she would sit with Mitchell until lunchtime. Lily said she would organise a hire car and would pick her up about 12.30pm then they would go for lunch. "After lunch can we go out to the property?" asked Leila.

This was the perfect time for Lily to call Queenstown and try to make contact with Mitchell's mother, as she would have no idea he was in hospital. Luck was with her, as her call was answered. "Hello Sarah, my name is Lily. I am calling from the Gold Coast in Australia. Your son Mitchell is in hospital in an induced coma as he is very ill. My daughter is his partner and she is by his side. I think you should come over as soon as possible as he is poorly."

"I haven't been in contact with Mitchell for years. His father would not let me contact him. What happened?" she asked.

Lily explained as best she could.

"But I don't have the money for an air ticket, as I have just come back from an overseas holiday."

Lily told her she would book her a flight and pay for it from the Australian end. She would just have to come at the earliest she could get a flight, if that suited. Sarah was grateful for Lily's offer and, yes, she was available anytime.

"I will do the booking, then call you and let you know the details."

Lily picked Leila up from the hospital and they went for lunch at a little café. She asked how Mitchell was, but there was no change. "The nurse told me they are worried he might have brain damage. What will I do if this is so? I don't think I love him enough to care for him full-time, but I can't abandon him."

Lily certainly didn't want Leila to tie her life up with Mitchell as he carried his father's stigma. Now that it was out in the neighbourhood about his father being a paedophile, where was this going to end up? Already his home was burnt down and he was attacked. The sooner she could get Leila away from all this the better. But how was the big question confronting her.

They drove out to the acreage and were not prepared for what confronted them. All that was left were charred ruins of what was once their home. Leila was shocked. There was her whole life gone, there was nothing left except the burnt shell, all her photos and her memories were lying among the ruins somewhere, probably charred bits of ash by now. It was in this moment she realised her past life here had come to an end. While they were standing looking at the ruins, their concentration was broken by a lady interrupting their silence. "Did you know the people who lived here?" she asked.

Leila answered first, "Yes as a matter of fact we did, and that was a shocking thing that happened to the young man. Look at their home. Why would anyone do such a terrible injustice? They were a young couple just starting out in life, now they have nothing," she fired back.

"But someone told us he was a paedophile, so we told the neighbourhood to be careful."

This was enough, and Leila let fly, "That is a lie. He is a forensic scientist and had just shifted over from Canada, but now he is lying in an induced coma fighting for his life. I hope whoever did this is severely punished."

On hearing this the lady didn't linger, and was quickly scurrying across the paddock. Was it her husband who was the culprit? Lily stood with her arms around Leila and they both stared at what was once a home that was now reduced to a burnt-out hovel. "Let's go, Mother. I can't stay here any longer. This is goodbye to my past. I have lost one family and gained another. My future is ahead of me."

Lily would like to have believed this was true, but where did Mitchell fit in?

As they were driving back to the motel, Lily told Leila they had a guest coming to stay, who they had to pick up at the Robina station tomorrow at 11.30am.

Lily dropped Leila off at the hospital, as she wanted to be with Mitchell in case there was some good news. This was not a bad idea, as Lily would have time to explain to Sarah what the situation was between Leila and Mitchell. As she pulled up at the station, several people were standing there waiting to be picked up and Lily had no idea which one was Sarah. She got out of the car and called her name. A lady came forward and held out her hand. "Hello Lily, I'm Sarah. Thank you for being so kind.

How is Mitchell?" she enquired. Lily explained there had been no improvement, and that Leila was at his bedside. "How did your daughter meet Mitchell?" she asked. How was Lily meant to explain this? It was so complicated, and besides she might not want to hear what she was going to be told. But she had to know the truth, in case anything embarrassing was said in front of Leila.

"I'm sorry that you have to hear this, Sarah, but better now than later. I know nothing about your life with your ex-husband, but a little over two years ago he raped my daughter who was only seventeen. He was her mentor at the surf lifesaving club. He drugged her and abandoned her in a boatshed down on the beach. A pregnancy followed and a little girl was born called Willow.

"Leila suffered such embarrassment, as she didn't know who the father was, and she had no idea who did this terrible act to her. It wasn't until she received a letter from a solicitor to say he had passed away and Willow and Mitchell were joint beneficiaries of his estate that the truth was revealed. There were nearly twenty-six years' difference in their ages. My daughter was shocked when this was revealed as she had put her trust in him. The solicitor did the negotiating between the two beneficiaries, but as Willow was only sixteen months, Leila acted as her guardian. Mitchell was in Canada finishing his studies, so it was suggested that Leila move into the property until he came back to Australia. This is how the friendship began."

Sarah was in shock: she couldn't speak, tears ran down her cheeks as she listened to what her ex had done. A young teenager, what the hell was he thinking, what could she say? It wasn't the shock of his philandering ways; it was the age of the victim. This took her back to her life with this man and bad memories came flooding back. She had put up with his affairs for years until one day she had had enough. Sadly, she had to leave without Mitchell, as she was not allowed to take him with her. Her husband paid her off, giving her enough money to buy a home on condition she broke all ties with Mitchell. She had no other choice!

"Are you okay?" asked Lily, as Sarah had sat in silence while thinking back over parts of her life.

"I'm so sad this happened to your Leila. In fact it makes me feel ashamed."

Lily stressed it was not Sarah's fault. "You are not responsible for his mistakes; he knew what he was doing was wrong. He obviously didn't think of the consequences or the embarrassment it caused Leila."

"Where is Willow now?" asked Sarah.

This was another long story that had to be told. It was all too much for Sarah. Such sadness and heartache; how did Leila cope with one disaster after another? She reached for Lily's hand and held it tight. A long silence followed. It was Sarah who spoke first. "Thank you for explaining everything, Lily. It is better I know before meeting Leila. ... Are Mitchell and Leila an item?"

Lily wasn't quite sure what the situation was, but she felt she had to let Sarah know how she felt. "I don't think it would be a good relationship, given it was Mitchell's father who raped Leila. Because it was known that a paedophile lived next door, someone bashed Mitchell and burnt the home down, so I don't want Leila mixed up in any of this; she doesn't deserve any more grief. We want her to come back to New Zealand and begin a new life with her family." Again, another bout of silence.

Sarah felt that Lily didn't want Mitchell and Leila to be together, but what if he needed her? The fact that his father was the paedophile wasn't Mitchell's fault.

At the hospital Lily led the way to Michell's ward. Standing outside the door was Leila and she was crying. "What is wrong my darling?" asked Lily.

"Mitchell needed to be hooked up to more oxygen as his breathing was deteriorating, so they asked me to wait outside."

It was then the introductions were done. Sarah said, "Your mother has told me what has happened, Leila. I'm sorry to hear you have gone through so much unneeded pain. You are a very brave young lady and Mitchell is lucky to have you by his side."

This did not go down at all well with Lily, as she wanted to discourage any pending relationship between Mitchell and Leila. "Yes, he needs me," Leila replied.

Lily had to bite her tongue for fear of saying something she might regret. The nurse appeared at the right time, to say they could go in to see Mitchell, but he was still unresponsive.

Sarah got a shock; she couldn't believe this was her son as she had not seen him for eighteen years, and to see him in this state was heart wrenching. She took his hand and held on to it, trying to coax him to give some sign that he knew her, but no response was forthcoming.

Another three days passed before there was any interaction from Mitchell, and this was in the way of a smile. His eyes opened for a few minutes then closed again. For the next two days this happened more often, as the nursing staff were pleased to note.

Today Lily talked Leila into having a break from the hospital, so they dropped Sarah there to sit with Mitchell. She wanted to take her shopping, to spoil her for all she had endured. They were having a lovely time until they passed a baby shop. Here Leila stopped and peered in the window. There was something like the last little romper suit she had bought Willow, so the memories came flooding back. "Mother, I just want to buy something in memory of Willow, please come with me," she asked. They went into the shop and she went straight to the romper suit and picked it up. "This is the last thing I bought Willow; I have to have this." So, she took it up to the counter.

"Is this a gift? Would you like it wrapped?" asked the assistant.

"No, it is for my little girl," replied Leila with tears running down her face.

"How old is she?"

At that, Leila burst into sobs. "She is dead."

The assistant looked stunned. Lily came to the rescue and thanked her and took the parcel, then put her arms around Leila and led her to a seat outside the shop so they could sit down. "I'm sorry, Mother if I embarrassed you. I don't know what came over me," she apologised.

Lily explained that this was not unexpected. "You will have moments like this for a long time to come when you will be overcome with grief. It is part of the grieving process. It is natural to miss a loved one, even if they have only been in your life for a short period of time."

They decided to call off the shopping and head back to the hospital at Leila's request.

As they entered Mitchell's ward, Sarah stood up and asked Leila to come and sit by Mitchell as he had been asking for her.

"What did he say?" she asked.

"He wanted to know where his girlfriend was. He didn't recognise me, so I never said anything as I didn't want to confuse him. I said you would be back soon."

After a short deliberation, Lily and Sarah decided to leave Leila with Mitchell and they would go back to the motel.

The following afternoon the hospital called to say Mitchell was awake and was asking for Leila. Could she please come and visit him? All three drove to the hospital. Lily wanted to be there to see what Mitchell remembered about their friendship. He was propped up in bed and when he saw Leila, he put his arms out and she went to him.

"I miss you, Leila, please don't leave me," he pleaded. His face was still swollen and bruised and the tubes were still attached to his body; he did not look well.

Lily asked him if he knew who their guest was. He

looked at Sarah blankly, but no, he didn't recognise her. It was Sarah who spoke. "I am your mother, Mitchell. Your father wouldn't let me have any contact with you when I left him, but I never stopped thinking about you. I moved to New Zealand so he couldn't contact me."

Mitchell looked at Sarah and couldn't believe she was his mother. "How did you know I was here?" he asked.

Sarah told him that Lily had contacted her to let her know her son was in hospital. "I don't want my father's name ever mentioned in my company. This is because of him," he said as he pointed to his face. "Leila and I have lost all our treasures when the home was torched, again because of him. I hate that man," he shouted.

This brought a nurse scurrying in to see what was wrong. "Please don't let Mitchell get upset. He is still very ill."

Leila took his hand and patted it until he calmed down. "Mother and I will wait outside so you can talk with your mother," she told him.

Sarah went over to sit by her son. She wanted to apologise for her absence from his life.

"Why did you leave me?" he asked.

"I left because your father was having affairs. He stopped loving me when I couldn't produce him with a child."

"What about me?" he interrupted.

Sarah continued to tell him he was adopted. "Did he not tell you?" she asked.

"That means I don't have his genes. Do you know what he did to Leila?"

Sarah nodded.

"That's how we met. Leila's daughter Willow was my half-sister. Now I love Leila, but her mother doesn't want us to be together and I can understand why. It is because of his stigma."

Sarah reassured him that because he was adopted, and not his biological son, none of his father's genes were passed on to him. "Don't beat yourself up. You are not his biological son, Mitchell, and you are not responsible for his shocking behaviour. This was on his head alone."

"He has ruined my life. I couldn't get a position with the Queensland police because of his reputation. They looked into his background and there was a black mark against his name, as he was noted as a paedophile. He has caused me no end of pain."

Sarah was full of apologies for the heartache her ex had caused. Mitchell thanked her for coming to Australia to see him. "How long are you staying?" he asked.

Sarah didn't know as she explained her funds were low as she had just come back from a six-week holiday abroad. Mitchell told her he would top up her bank account as he had money. She thanked him and said she would pay him back when she went to work. "There are plenty of cleaning jobs in Queenstown because it is a popular tourist destination."

Mitchell looked at his mother and couldn't think of her as a cleaning person, tidying up after other people; she deserved better than that. "I don't want you doing housekeeping work, but we will talk about that at a later date. First, I have to get better. I haven't been told what my prognosis is, so we will ask the doctor together. I may need someone to care for me for a while, as I haven't been out of bed yet. I have been thinking, I will encourage Leila to go back to New Zealand with her mother as we are homeless, and I will visit her when I'm better. I will miss her, but I can't be selfish."

As he spoke Sarah could see his eyes were misty. She knew he had feelings for Leila, but the stigma of his father was still raw. She could understand a lot of Lily's thinking on a long-term relationship, and whether this stigma would always be present, especially if there was stress between them. This was the unknown.

Today the doctor wanted a family meeting. He had all his reports and X-rays to explain what physical and psychological injuries could come from this brutal attack. The doctor told them that psychological effects can be devastating, and the victim may experience fear, anxiety, depression, anger, guilt and shame. Until he was up and walking any of these could side-track him. There were still two machines attached to him and they were going to be coming off over the next few days, providing he continued on his uphill climb. As yet, his mobility had not been tested.

"Mitchell's physical injuries mean he may suffer memory and concentration problems, isolation, avoidance and flashbacks. We have kept him pretty well sedated to avoid these problems occurring, allowing him to heal, but we will gradually decrease his medication and watch to see if he can overcome them himself. His body has to learn to fight back on its own accord, so mentally this is going to be a huge challenge. We are going to send him to a rehabilitation centre, where he will receive physio care that will hopefully help him regain his strength and self-belief. He will spend about six months there and then we will reassess him. Mitchell will need a support person with him for this time. There is no reason he won't make a full recovery, but he has many hurdles to jump before that happens. He will be here for a further two weeks, before he starts his rehabilitation. I can't elaborate any further as we don't know what's ahead. It's up to Mitchel to set himself goals and work hard to achieve them."

When the doctor left the ward, everyone sat in silence. They were all taken back by what they had been told: such a long recovery time with no assurances all would be okay in the end. It was Sarah who broke the silence. "I will be Mitchell's support person. I owe that to him."

This brought a protest from Leila, who offered her time, saying she should be the one caring for him. Lily sat back and bit her tongue, as no way did she want Leila to suffer any more. She was young and had a career ahead of her.

It was Mitchell who had the final say and agreed that it was his mother's place to be his support person. "I want you to go back to New Zealand, Leila, to be with your family and when I am well again, I will come for you. We having nothing left here, only bad memories."

While they were talking, a police officer entered the ward. He told them he had been assigned to Mitchell's case, but he had waited until the victim was able to cope being questioned.

"Can you tell me what happened on the night of the attack?" he asked. Mitchell looked at him. He hadn't yet even gone back there in his thoughts, and now that he tried to remember his mind was a blank. Was this the beginning of his memory and concentration problems?

"Did you see your attacker?" was the next question. Again, he couldn't offer any explanation; perhaps his mind was blocking out the traumatic experience. Would he ever remember? Perhaps he was not meant to.

The next questions followed, "Was there a reason for this attack? Had you had a falling out with your neighbour? Did you upset him?"

Mitchell was getting annoyed. He explained he had not long ago come back from Canada and had only moved in recently and hadn't met any of his neighbours. Once again, he felt a victim of his father's crime, but how could he tell the officer with Leila in the room? He didn't want to embarrass her.

Sarah had listened to this conversation and spoke up in defence of Mitchell. "The property originally belonged to Mitchell's father who turned out to be a paedophile. He has since died, so Leila and Mitchell lived there. He is not responsible for his father's past, so this was a horrible injustice."

The officer then asked if the father's victim was a neighbour's child. Lily's gaze immediately went to Leila, who jumped up and ran out of the room. This brought to light what Lily already knew in her own heart, that there was going to be an ongoing resentment every time this subject came up. How could a relationship work between

Mitchell and Leila? It was doomed before it started, and in her mind it was not a healthy base for any relationship.

Now it was Mitchell who spoke up. "No the victim was not a neighbour; the victim has just left the room. My so-called father has ruined my life. But I have just been told he was not my biological father, so I have none of his bad blood."

This was the first Lily knew of this. Would it change her mind about him, as this ruled out her theory of him inheriting his father's genes? But it didn't change the situation in her eyes.

The police officer told Mitchell they had the neighbour in custody, but he was going to be let out on bail, until he was charged. He would keep him up to date on what was happening right through the investigation. As he left the room, he met Leila in tears in the hospital corridor. "I'm sorry, I had no idea you were the victim. Forgive me for causing you grief."

This confirmed to Leila that she had to get as far away as possible from all this.

Today Leila and Lily were visiting Mitchell for the last time before they flew out to New Zealand. He was free from all machines, but he still looked very weak. His body had taken a terrible bashing, with broken ribs and cracked bones in his upper body, so the next six months were going to be a battle he was determined to win. "I'll get better and come to New Zealand for you, Leila," he told her.

This did not escape Lily's ears. Leila bent over and kissed him goodbye, and Lily heard him tell her he loved her. All she could hope for was the separation would have a negative influence on their relationship. Lily shook Mitchell's hand and wished him a speedy recovery; she couldn't not wish him well. Sarah promised to keep in touch with Leila on Mitchell's rehabilitation progress.

The next stop was at the university for Leila to sign off and pick up her papers as to the levels she had reached in her law studies. The registrar understood Leila's plight and told her to keep up the good work as she was excelling in her studies.

At the airport all the family including Reece were waiting for their flight to land. Lily and Leila had flown into Christchurch then caught an internal flight to Dunedin. As they made their way through arrivals, it was now only a matter of time before the reunions started. There were hugs all around as once again they were reunited as a family, this time forever. Leila was going to live with Reece as he was on his own and they had a good rapport. It was like the days he remembered, when she cried and begged him to stay each time he left to fly back to Auckland.

Lily was happy with these arrangements as she felt Reece had missed out on a lot over the past few years. Now he was rewarded. They all drove back to Reece's home and celebrated a happy family get-together. After a few days of relaxation Lily would take Leila to Otago University and get her enrolled, as she had already spoken to the registrar, so they were expecting her. Lily had offered her a job in her spare time, to begin as a junior at her law firm, as this would help her immensely with her studies, and she would be getting the practical work along with her lectures.

Harrison had coaxed Leila into the gaming world, so it was not unusual for her to arrive home late, but she kept this to a Friday and Saturday night. She, like Lily, was taking extra night classes to further her studies, hoping to get her degree with higher qualifications. He was introducing her to lots of young people her own age, which opened up a whole new horizon to her. She thought of Mitchell less and less as her life was so busy.

Sarah, as promised, was keeping them up to speed on Mitchell's progress. He had lost his self-esteem and still carried his father's guilt on his shoulders. But one little ray of sunshine was he had become friendly with one of his nurses, so he was putting a lot of trust in her. The less he thought about Leila, the less the problem of his father's crime became apparent. Sarah had now realised that Lily's way of thinking may have some merit after all. She realised perhaps Mitchell and Leila's relationship would be better as a friendship rather than anything more.

Two years on

In Australia, Mitchell had finished his rehabilitation and was back to his fit, healthy self. Sarah had sold her home in Queenstown and moved back to the Gold Coast to be near her son. He had reapplied for a position as a forensic scientist with the Queensland police and was accepted. Because of his recent association with the police regarding his assault and the arson of his home, they found him to be a reliable person. He kept in touch with Leila, although only on a friendship level, as he was dating his physio nurse and it all seemed to be going along fine.

Meanwhile Leila had settled into her new life and was loving every moment. She grew close to Lily who she now regarded as her new mother and Reece as her father. Mackenzie and Harrison were her siblings, no half measures, but full siblings. The one person she had taken a shine to was Lincoln. He was so different to what was the norm, but sadly he was old enough to be her father. In fact she had managed to get him out of his home on several occasions, to talk to the students at university. Lily was a bit on edge with this friendship, as there would be no future there if she wanted to have children; he just wasn't that sort of person. She hoped it was just a passing phase she was going through!

The fortunes of the three lads had gone up three-fold and now they were at their highest peak … they were billionaires. Their shares in the gaming company had jumped from $1.20 to $24.00 a share. Harrison had sold their new game to all his online gamers all over the world, thus pushing the shares to their highest price. He was rewarded handsomely by Lincoln's company, as he was now employed as a gaming programmer on a very high salary. Their virtual land was moving slowly, but that potential was still a little way off. It was the gaming industry that had accelerated and would continue to do so. The big question: to sell or not to sell? Decisions would have to be made.

Lily was busy for the next week as she was the judge on a case where three young men were appearing before the court for supplying alcohol with intent to seduce young girls. This case was of interest to Leila, so she asked Lily if she could attend court each day instead of going to work. Varsity had finished for their two-week break, so it worked out well. The three young men were in fact fifteen and sixteen-year-olds, but old enough to know that to get girls drunk while playing a game called 'roll the dice' would lead to trouble. One of the girls ended up pregnant, so had to explain to her parents how it happened. It was the parents who reported this to the police, who had to act. The girls were willing participants, but the question was whether they consented to having sex, or were their visions blurred by alcohol, and who supplied drink to these underage teenagers.

Leila took notes each day, as to her this was 'close to home' – she had been there. She took a very dim view of males who took advantage of young girls and women, when they weren't capable of consenting to having sex. This took her back to what Amelia must have suffered in her own home by her one guardian. Leila felt she was batting for herself and Amelia, as the two people they had trusted in their lives took advantage of them. It was not a male's right to just presume he could please himself, when the other person was not in control of making good decisions. It was utter selfishness on their behalf.

Throughout the case the young men could not see that they were responsible for their actions, as it always came back to the girls agreeing to play the game. As Lily listened to the blame game, she was disappointed that none of the lads could see that the alcohol had affected the girls' ability to make sound decisions. As the dice was rolled and a six came up, a swig from the bottle of vodka was taken, along with an item of clothing to be removed. The first person to become naked was then allowed to pick a partner and leave the room with them for a 'kiss and cuddle' session. But the boys took this as an invitation to complete their mission and this was where the line was overstepped.

At the end of the hearing, Lily had to sum up the case before her. That the girls had taken part in the game, thinking it was innocent fun, led Lily to believe that it was just a game to them, not a full-on agreement that allowed the boys to rob them of their innocence. When alcohol was introduced by the boys, it gave them the power to bed the girls without a clear consent from them. If alcohol had not been involved, it may well have been a very different outcome. On this alone, Lily found the boys guilty for what happened; the girls were taken advantage of under the influence of alcohol. It transpired that the alcohol was bought by the boys, from friends who had been involved in 'smash n grab' raids who wanted a quick buck to buy drugs.

The boys were sentenced to 200 hours each of community work and if they appeared before the court again within a year, they would end up in a detention centre. Leila wished the penalty had been harsher than what they received, but as Lily explained, the girls were willing to shed their clothes on the role of a dice, in mixed company. As Leila thought about this, yes, the temptation was there. This case could not be compared to her and Amelia's as they were innocent victims without a say.

Leila learned a lot today, that not all rape cases could be treated the same. This was good grounding for her, as it opened her eyes to the fact that each case must be treated on its own merit, not to be locked in as a 'one for all' punishment. Leila had tremendous respect for Lily as she handled everything in a calm, collected manner, which was why she had earned her appointment as a High

Court judge, as she remained neutral and saw both sides of each case.

Leila was visiting Lincoln today as she promised to cook him dinner. She told Reece she would be home late, not to wait up for her. When he found out she was going to Lincoln's he rang Lily and asked her if there was something going on, as she had been visiting him a lot recently. "I have reservations about that friendship, but what can we do? I didn't know if she could ever love a man after what happened to her, but she told me she could, if she met the right one. Surely, she hasn't got feelings for Lincoln. He's nearly your age, Reece. Oh my God, tell me it's not true. Her mentor who stole her innocence was a middle-aged man, so why would she go there?

"Leave it with me and I will speak to Kennedy. Perhaps he will talk with Lincoln on the quiet.

That night as Lily climbed into bed, she brought up the subject of Leila and Lincoln. "Do you think Lincoln might be interested in Leila?"

"Funny you should say that. He has been really happy lately and is taking an interest in his appearance. Leila has even got him out of his home to speak at the varsity. He never left his property for months, so why now?"

Kennedy wondered if Leila carried the same warmth as her mother. Then he could understand how Lincoln felt, as it was something very special that only a few people experienced.

"Reece rang to say Leila was cooking him tea tonight and she wouldn't be home till late. He is worried. I can't believe she would even entertain the idea of an older man. You don't think she has something to prove to herself? I hope this isn't revenge for her and Amelia's suffering?" replied Lily.

Kennedy agreed to speak with Lincoln in the morning. Here was Lily, still the mother figure to everyone. That was why he loved her as much today as when he first met her. It was that warmth she possessed, which flowed through to him, making him want to hold her close to his heart. Their love for each other had never waned; it was still alive and well, and he could still arouse her with his caresses. They were very much the lovers today that they were at the start of their affair.

Kennedy decided to call in on Lincoln on his way to work and was surprised to find Leila there. His first thought, had she spent the night with him? It wasn't right as he was only a couple of years younger than her father. Before he could hold his thoughts to himself, he found himself asking, "What are you doing here this early?"

Lincoln heard him and came to the door. "We spent the night together. Don't be angry with us as we have talked it over. We wanted to see if it could work, and it's early days yet. I never expected to ever have another partner, but on touching Leila, something changed within me. I know Lily and Reece will hate me for this. I will speak with them and explain, but Reece will know something already, as Leila never went home last night.

"I asked Leila to think hard before anything happened between us, as I am not your ordinary run of the mill sort of person. I'm a tech nerd but she has accepted that. Don't worry, a lot of discussion has taken place, and I still can't believe I feel this way about her; she is a special person, her warmth is something else."

Kennedy was lost for words. All these years they had known each other … this couldn't possibly be happening. It wasn't right him loving Reece and Lily's daughter; where was the logic in that? But then logic didn't come into the equation. He knew from experience that love won out above all else, and if Leila had inherited Lily's warmth, then he could understand why Lincoln was drawn to her. The only hiccup he could see was the twenty-five year age gap. How was Lily going to accept this? He would wait until tonight when they were cuddled up in bed before he broke the news to her as he could foresee tears coming and plenty of them. She would need comforting. As Lily had mentioned, did she have something to prove to herself? It was a complicated affair and only time would tell. Was this the end of a long friendship, one that had spanned many years?

Tonight, when Kennedy arrived home from work, he noticed Reece's car parked at his gate. He had a feeling he knew why Reece was there. As he walked in the door, he could hear raised voices and the loudest was Reece's. "Leila never came home last night; she must have stayed with Lincoln. Why the hell would she do that for, Lily?"

Lily was taken aback by this. No, Leila wouldn't have done that, surely. It was now time for Kennedy to step in with the truth. "Yes, Leila spent the night with Lincoln as they are an item. Last night was a trial run to see if things can work out between them."

This brought an outcry from Reece. "He's old enough to be her father. What is he thinking? This is ridiculous, our daughter and our friend. No way will I allow this," he bellowed.

Lily was just as flabbergasted. "How do you know this, Kennedy?" she asked.

He told her when he called to see Lincoln this morning Leila opened the door. It was then that Lincoln told him of his feelings for her.

"What did you say?" roared Reece.

"What could I say? They are grown adults making their own decisions. Whatever we say will make no difference, it won't change anything." The three of them stood and stared at each other. Lily burst into tears; this is not what she wanted for Leila. Reece was furious. "I will tell Lincoln to stay away from her. She is still a child."

Kennedy pointed out to Reece that Leila was of an age to make her own decisions and if he interfered, he would drive her away. "Just let it be in the meantime. It may not work out, but they are giving it a go. Please don't try and stop them as it will only make things worse; you have her back after all these years so be thankful for that, I beg of you, Reece."

Lily found herself agreeing with Kennedy. There was nothing they could do but wait it out and hope the age difference would divide them. Reece was not convinced, but then that was in his nature, and when it came to understanding a family problem, he was hopeless. There was always blame.

"How am I going to feel if Leila wants to move in with

Lincoln?" asked Reece.

"You will just have to accept her decision," said Kennedy. "We have to put our feelings aside and remain unbiased on what she chooses to do. Remember she has not had our guidance in her life, so we don't know how she thinks. Her life has been far from normal, so we have to make provisions for that, Reece. If we go in 'guns-a blazing' we will drive her away. Let us be supportive of her and hope whatever happens we will be there for her."

Reece was sad to think he might lose her, and he would be on his own again, alone in the family home. But Lincoln! He couldn't get his head around this; what would Leila find attractive about him? Okay, he had brains, but he was different to most other men. He had become an introvert since Covid reared its ugly head. What would he say to him when they next met? Could he be civil? He didn't know. But his biggest worry was Leila and how he would react to her when she came home. He wished it was all a bad dream and would just disappear!

As Reece was preparing his evening meal, in walked Leila. "Hi, Father, how was your day?" she asked.

Rage had been boiling away in his mind all day. "My day was fine. How was yours?" he replied. Leila sensed his curt tone and knew by this that he had heard the news. She asked him to come and sit down as she had something she wanted him to know. Before she could get out her next sentence, Reece beat her to it. "Why Lincoln of all people? He's not right for you, Leila, he's nearly my age. What about a family? He is not a family man. What were you thinking?"

"I know you are upset and I don't blame you, but he lit a light in my heart, something I have never felt before. He is different, but that is not a reason why I shouldn't have feelings for him. We hit it off together; he is really quite quirky. As for a family, I had my little girl and she was taken from me."

This statement brought Reece to tears and his heart melted. "But you might feel different in a few years."

Leila stood up and went to Reece and hugged him. "Please, Father, accept what is happening for my sake. I enjoy Lincoln's company. We are working things out. I know not everyone will be happy, but both Lincoln and I are."

The next morning at work, Lily called Leila into her chambers. As Leila walked in, she got in first. "I know, Mother, you are not happy with my choice and I understand why, but my heart has been ripped from me several times. My life has been far from normal. I'm not your average daughter and I think differently."

"But, Leila, what about children? You're still young," replied Lily.

Leila's next statement stabbed Lily right in heart. "I had a little girl whom I struggled to love, as my maternal passion wasn't there, and I hated myself for that. Willow was more Amelia's little girl than mine. All I felt was guilt when I lost her, not love," she sobbed.

"But that is understandable my darling, you were raped, Willow was conceived out of an act of selfishness, not love. It was wrong, so it was hard for you to bond with her. That's not your fault. You won't always feel like that. Time is a great healer and teaches you to forget and forgive.

"If Lincoln is your choice, we will accept it. We love you, Leila, you are our daughter. And as you mentioned, your life has not been an easy ride, so enjoy what is ahead. Go back to work and don't worry about your father and me. Lincoln has always been part of our lives and always will. Reece, Kennedy and Lincoln are like brothers: they have hit highs and lows together, but they have always been there for each other. They have made their fortunes as friends and will continue to build the empire they dreamed about right from when I came on the scene. Nothing will sever their friendship, and Reece will come round in his own time. Think of this as a little hiccup that will just float out to sea and disappear. The waves will carry it away."

Lily's thoughts had now been confirmed. As Willow was not born out of love, Leila's feelings for her daughter had never materialised, so she was thankful, in a sad way, that she was taken along with Amelia. This left Leila with no reminders of her past life, so she could now start a new life from scratch, and if that was with Lincoln, then that's what it was. She and Reece would provide all their support from here on in.

Their little girl who was stolen had come back to them as a lovely young lady, and now it was their time to support and love her, no matter the trials and tribulations she brought with her. After all, she was still their beautiful Leila.

Also by Margaret Nyhon

FICTION

Isobella (Book 1 in the *Isobella* series)

Isobella: Self Redemption (Book 2 in the *Isobella* series)

Papa's Girl Emmeline

Betrayal by an Irish Rose

Revenge for an English Lord (sequel to *Betrayal by an Irish Rose*)

For Girls' Eyes Only

Daughters Lost to the Underworld

Pimchan and Amira

Coronavirus: A Novel

The Whistle-blower's Severed Link (sequel to *Coronavirus: A Novel*)

Fortune Smiles as Love Divides

The Stolen Girl

NON-FICTION

de Marisco

Freedom Knows No Boundaries

A Wake-up Call

A Shattered Dream Across the Tasman

Memories and Moving On

About the Author

Margaret Nyhon lives in Mosgiel, New Zealand, where she writes, paints and practises the crafts of printing and bookbinding.

She has worked extensively in hospitality management in New Zealand and resort management in Australia. The urge to trace her family history led her to the writing of her first non-fiction work, *de Marisco*. She has since written several fiction and non-fiction books. Margaret is married and has three adult children and two grandsons.

Contact Margaret: margaretf@hotmail.co.nz